THE VAMPYRES OF MONTEVIDEO

AND OTHER STRANGE TALES

THE VAMPYRES OF MONTEVIDEO

AND OTHER STRANGE TALES

By Gloria Hobson

Copyright © 2020 Gloria Hobson

All rights reserved.

The moral right of the author has been asserted.

ISBN: 9798564502863

Except where actual historical events and characters are being used for the storyline of this book, all situations in this publication are fictitious and any resemblance to living persons is purely coincidental.

Book cover design by Creative Covers

DEDICATION

For everyone who struggled during Lockdown 2020

Table of Contents

DEDICATION 5

The Vampyres of Montevideo 9

The Little Dutch Boy 13

A Handsome Piece 17

The Dead of Night 22

Fit For a King 25

The Demon 29

Can It Be Magic? 32

The Eye of the Beholder 39

A Holiday Tale 43

Willows 47

An Eye For An Eye 53

A Gift From Zaria 59

A Night on Pendle Hill 62

The Dentist 66

Pitter – Patter 71

A Day Out 75

Salvation 78

All Hallowes 82

Trick or Treat 83

The Scales of Justice 86

Let Sleeping Dogs Lie 92

The Waiting Room 96

The Rocker 98
Kismet 103
Once Bitten 108
The Doppleganger 117
The Army of Lost Souls 122
A Silver Lining 125
ABOUT THE AUTHOR 136

Gloria Hobson

The Vampyres of Montevideo

Hugo Smyth (or to give him his full name Hugo Vladimir Smyth) sank onto the rickety old bed with relief. It had been a long and tiring journey from Europe to Montevideo but it would be worth it he was sure

The small hotel was not up to his usual standard but he wanted to remain anonymous and this backstreet Pension would suffice for now. He would rest for a couple of hours and then explore the neighbourhood and see if it had the rich pickings he had been led to believe. Surely a city of over 3 million would offer potential for his new venture.

It was almost dark when Hugo awoke; he showered quickly, changed and went out onto the street. The Hotel El Cordoba was at the edge of a very busy square, lots of bars and cafes and that Friday night buzz which gave big cities a wonderful atmosphere. For a few pesos you could get tapas and a glass of wine and he chose a corner table where he could indulge in his favourite pastime : people watching.

His eyes settled on a particularly handsome waiter, dark features, white teeth and slim hips, not too tall and muscular, just what he was looking for. He sighed, too close to home, he would have to venture further afield, into the poorer quarters where missing persons would go unnoticed. For, you see, Hugo Smythe was a VAMPIRE, not the old fashioned Count Dracula type who slept in a coffin all day and who could only be killed with a stake through the heart, no, he was a thoroughly modern guy who was in dire need of a fresh supply of victims.

Some rumours were circulating about him in Europe and it was becoming too risky. He needed somewhere new, somewhere he could blend in with other foreigners, somewhere far from home and Uruguay was about as far as you could get.

Suddenly his eye was caught by some beggars wandering between the tables, a woman and two teenage boys. Searching in his pocket for some loose change he beckoned them over.

'Gracias Senor, muchas gracias,' the woman said, the money quickly disappearing into her ample bosom.

Hugo caught the eye of the older of the two boys and held his gaze for a few seconds. The boy blushed but nodded his head slightly. He knew certain men found him attractive and he could always use a few extra pesos. Hugo finished his drink, left some money on the table and followed him into the shadows, trailing behind as they meandered through the myriad of back streets and alleys. In a small courtyard the boy stopped and turned but before he could utter a sound Hugo held him in a fierce grip and sank his razor sharp fangs into his neck.

He drank his fill and felt his spirits lift as energy flowed into him and life flowed out of his victim.

Hiding the body behind some rubble in a dark corner Hugo the Vampire silently made his way back to his hotel, ready for a good night's sleep, well satisfied with his first encounter and looking forward to tomorrow when he thought he might pay a visit to an Art Gallery he had heard about.

The next few days passed in a pleasant haze, doing all the usual tourist things but by the end of the first week he was ready for another victim. Thinking it might save some money and give him more privacy, he visited a letting agent and viewed a few apartments before settling for one near the river. His next two victims were homeless boys, it was almost too easy, they were so eager to join him. Both bodies he disposed of in the river and watched as they floated out to sea on the strong tidal current.

Hugo settled into an agreeable routine. Usually one victim a week satisfied him especially young ones as their blood was much sweeter and cleaner. And then it happened. Trawling through the back streets near the market one night, he had the distinct feeling he was being followed, just a slight movement behind him, a shadow out of the corner of his eye, a prickling at the back of his neck.

He stepped into a doorway and peered into the darkness but could see nothing. Feeling slightly nervous he decided to return home and it was with a sigh of relief that he turned the key in the lock and stepped into his tiny living room.

Four men stood waiting for him, a reception committee you could say, but they seemed far from welcoming.

'Who are you?' he asked, 'how did you get in here?'

'We know who you are and what you are doing,' replied one of the men, 'we are here to warn you. We are the local faction, there is no room for outsiders here, especially foreigners, it is OUR territory.'

He stepped closer and smiled. Hugo could see the telltale teeth.

'We suggest you move on Senor.' With that they moved in unison out of the door, black capes flapping dramatically.

Well Hugo did not scare easily, it was usually him who did the scaring, nevertheless he would have to tread carefully. It did not pay to make enemies in this game. He would have to explore further afield, to the edge of the city, away from their territory. He would go by tram, it was only a few pesos, but he would need to be vigilant, off the tourist track this could be a dangerous city, many gangs roamed and murders were common.

A couple of nights later he set off, travelling to the northern terminus. This was a real 'favella' and people stared at him with open hostility. As he rounded a corner he was suddenly confronted by six young men.

'Buenos tardes,' he said in a friendly manner.
They looked at him in silence and there was a quick flash as one of them waved a knife in the air.

Discretion is the better part of valour, thought Hugo, even a vampire couldnt take on six at once. Better give them his wallet and he reached into his pocket. The one with the knife stepped forward and in one swift movement slashed Hugo across the throat.

'You were warned Amigo, you were warned,' said the knifeman as hot blood arched into the air and Hugo sank to his knees.

The six men knelt at his side lapping thirstily at the bright blood, like kittens round a saucer of milk.

Hugo's strength was slipping away as the gang feasted noisily on him and he knew death was close, how ironic that a vampire should die from lack of blood was his last thought as he closed his eyes and blackness overcame him.

His body was found the next morning and the Policia were summoned. The Chief looked down at him with pity in his eyes.

'Tourists, they wander off the beaten track and this is what happens. Those murders we had in the centre seem to have moved out here, better put out some extra patrols.'

He looked around.

'So little blood, how strange, perhaps we have a vampire amongst us, better order a fresh supply of garlic, eh, Sergeant?', he winked and they all laughed politely at his joke though many turned away and crossed themselves nervously.

The Little Dutch Boy

I first saw the little Dutch boy when I was about 10. I lived in Amsterdam with my family and every summer my mother packed me off to stay with my grandmama in her small cottage near Alkmaar, on the coast. It was quite a wild, bleak place with fierce winds blowing in from the North Sea and I loved it. I liked to sit in an old wicker chair on the front porch watching the waves crashing against the sea wall and the gulls screeching over head. I would read books, write a lot and sketch a little.

I saw the boy walking down the lane swinging a stick. His clothes seemed very threadbare and his clogs well worn and dirty. He was very thin.

I waved and he waved back. Grandmama said no one knew his name or where he came from, some said he was abandoned as a baby and lived in the poor house, others that he was orphaned when his parents died in the floods of '48. Some even said he was a sea wraith come to haunt us, a ghostly spectre destined to walk the foreshore forever, like a landlocked 'Flying Dutchman'.

To me he just seemed like a hungry child and I felt very sorry for him.

I took some pickled herrings from the kitchen and walked across to sit next to him on the sea wall.

'Hello, I'm Freda,' I said, 'what's your name?' No reply. I held out the fish. 'would you like these?.

He took them slowly and ate in silence.

'I live across there with my grandmama' I pointed to the little white washed cottage. ' where do you live?'

He gazed out to sea wistfully and made no reply, bored I wandered home for tea.

That night there was a terrible storm which raged until dawn when it finally blew itself out. Across the sand dunes were strewn all manner of flotsam and jetsom brought in on the tide. I could make out a tiny figure clambering amongst the wreckage. I stood on the porch and watched as the boy dragged some old timbers back onto the pathway. I put on my coat and went to help him.

'What are you going to make? I asked, not expecting a reply.

'A boat,' he said, much to my surprise, 'I need to get home, I need to see my mother and sisters.'

'And where is that?' I asked

'Oh, over there,' he replied, vaguely waving his arm towards the sea. 'Will you help me?.

'Of course,' I said.

All week we laboured, I searched in Grandpapas old shed for a hammer and nails, anything that would help and finally we had something resembling a flat bottomed boat that did not seem at all seaworthy. Of course, I didn't really expect him to actually use it, it was just a bit of childish fun, we could sit in it on the beach and pretend to be sailors. He seemed very pleased with it and even managed to construct a small sail out of some ragged pieces of cloth he found on the shore. We parted feeling we had done a good days work.

Next morning, after breakfast, I went out to look for my little nameless friend but he was nowhere to be found, the boat was missing too. I waited and walked along the foreshore all day but he didn't appear. The following day was the same and the one after and eventually I had to admit that he was gone and I would probably never see him again.

Well, the summer passed and I thought of him often, wondering what had become of him. Eventually the time to return to the city drew close and on the last day I decided to go for one last walk. It was a fine blustery day so I thought I would venture as far as the cliffs around the headland to the north. They were not very high but there were a couple of caves and plenty of rock pools to explore.

As I poked about looking for crabs I heard a slight rumbling above me and suddenly a voice cried out

'Freda, look out!' and running around the headland appeared the little Dutch boy, he launched himself at me and pushed me violently away from the cliff face. I fell face down into the sandy gravel as a huge boulder came crashing down, missing me by inches. I lay there stunned for a moment, then I managed to stand up and brush myself down. My knees were slightly bloodied but I knew immediately that, if the rock had hit me, I would probably be dead.

I looked around for my friend to thank him but he had disappeared yet again. What a strange child, I thought as I staggered home.

Grandmama fussed as only grandmamas can. She bathed my knee and made hot chocolate as I related my adventure to her.

'And if the little Dutch boy hadn't pushed me out of the way, goodness knows what might have happened,' I concluded.

Grandmama paled, 'the little Dutch boy?' She started to tremble. 'that can't be.'

'Why?' I asked, puzzled.

She produced a newpaper.

'I bought this in the town this morning,' she replied, handing it over to me. 'Read it.'

I took it from her and looked down at the main story. I can still remember the exact words even now, 20 years later.

The decomposed body of a young boy was found on the beach near Den Helder yesterday. It is thought to be 8 year old Thomas van Hoorn, one of only four survivors from the

Gloria Hobson

ferry disaster two years ago that killed his mother and twin sisters. Nearby was the wreckage of a small boat.

I went outside to sit in my chair on the porch, looking out to sea, silent tears streaming down my face.

Poor Thomas, he had gone searching for his beloved family and now he had found them and they were reunited .

But he came back for one last visit, to save me and I'll never forget him, I will always remember him, my friend, the Little Dutch Boy

A Handsome Piece

It was one of those cool Autumn days towards the end of October, quite pleasant in the thin sunshine but with a nip in the air which foretold of the winter to come. Crisp dry leaves were scudding across the High Street, swirling down from the tall beech trees which lined the pavement, the sweet odour of burning leaves settled gently over the town.

Tucked away between the boot repairers and the butchers was a small antique shop, owned and managed by Miss May Campbell, a petite, tidy lady of indeterminate age. She had bought the business five years ago and, though the profits were marginal, it created a pleasant diversion in what was an otherwise lonely, slightly tedious life

She lived in the small flat above which she had made very cosy and comfortable with the help of some of the nicer pieces she came across at the many sales she attended. Like most people living alone, May Campbell had settled into a pedantic routine; she rose at 7.30 and, wearing an old woolen dressing gown, she first went into her tiny kitchen and put the kettle on. While waiting for that to boil she would feed Jenny, her large tabby cat, and then she would pad downstairs to collect the papers. She would eat two slices of toast with honey and at 8.30 she would dress and be ready to open the shop at 9.00 o'clock

Except for Thursdays that is. On Thursdays she would usually go to one of the local antique sales or occasionally would visit people in their homes who rang to say they had someting of interest to sell. It was on one such visit that she first met Tom Stone.

Gloria Hobson

He rang one Wednesday to say he had an oak table he wished to dispose of and, as he lived in the next village only 6 miles away, she told him she would call on Thursday morning. She found his cottage quite easily and parked her battered old blue van on the grass verge.

Tom Stone turned out to be a widower in his late fifties, a tall handsome man with a slight stoop. He had what could best be described as old world charm and yet there was a coldness in his eyes that she found a little unsettling. He invited her in with a theatrical sweep of his arm.

The table was certainly worth the journey, a very heavy, ornately carved oak refectory table that was in excellent condition apart from three small notches on the inside of one leg, but they were hardly noticeable except to the trained eye and in no way detracted from its charm. Her offer was accepted immediately and as she wrote out the cheque, she felt a glow of satisfaction at a job well done.

With the aid of a small trolley which she always carried with her, they were able to manhandle it into the van, the springs groaning in protest at the sudden extra weight. When Tom Stone asked her if she would like some tea, while normally she would politely refuse, he was so insistent that on this occasion she murmured acceptance.

It was a very pretty sitting room, full of china ornaments and bric-a-brac, obviously a lifetimes collection, perhaps the legacy of his late wife she thought. The chintzy curtains and hand embroidered cushion covers gave it a very feminine feel and yet, as she sipped her tea and looked about her discreetly, the one thing she could not see were any photographs. She found this quite puzzling, most people of his generation had quite a collection, wedding groups, children, grandchildren, that type of thing. Still, it was none of her business and she quickly dismissed it from her mind.

Miss Campbell drank her tea, they talked about antiques and the approaching winter and within a quarter of an hour she had bade him goodbye and headed eagerly back to town.

The rest of the morning was spent clearing a space for the table, she wanted it to have pride of place in the window, it was such a handsome piece. She had to commandeer the butchers boy to help get it inside but it certainly looked splendid when it was in position. For added effect she laid six places with a beautiful Sevres dinner service and, as she stood back to admire it, May Campbell had to admit, with a certain pride, that it had been a good morning's work.

Next day at 10.30 the phone rang. It was Tom Stone enquiring after some large brass candlesticks and when she told him she had quite a selection, he said he would call shortly and sure enough, within half an hour he came through the door. After making his purchase he asked if anyone had yet shown any interest in the table and Miss Campbell said that she had noticed a few people looking in the window but no one had actually been in.

He seemed surprised at that but of course it was early days she explained, hers was not a fast turnover, sometimes she had things for years before they were sold, she hardly exected to sell the table immediately! Looking slightly disappointed, Tom Stone left.

His car had barely pulled away from the kerb when a smartly dressed, middle aged lady who looked vaguely familiar, entered the shop and headed straight for the table. She spent a lot of time examining the intricate carving which was certainly very beautiful and she was especially interested in its history. Of course, apart from telling her it was purchased locally, there was not a great deal Miss Campbell could impart though she did say she might be able to put her in touch with the previous owner if he was in agreement. She didn't think it quite proper to divulge information without express consent, so she made a mental note to ring Tom Stone later.

The lady agreed to call back the following day and, casting a last glance towards the table, strode out of the door, the bell tinkling merrily behind her.

That evening Miss Campbell spoke to Mr Stone on the telephone and he seemed most excited at the news of a prospective buyer; he wanted to know all about her, her name, appearance, age, in fact anything she could recall. She thought it a little odd but told him all she could and, of course, he said he would be only too pleased to meet the lady, the sooner, the

better. Miss Campbell was quite at liberty to give her his name and address.
This she duly did the next day, the lady paying cash and making her own arrangements to have it collected later in the afternoon. Miss Campbell was quite sad to see it go so soon, naturally she was pleased to sell it, after all it was her livelihood but it was so splendid she would have liked to have had it in her shop a little longer, to savour it, so to speak.

Well, she thought no more about it and life went on much the same until, about six weeks later, she picked up her copy of the local newpaper and there, on the middle pages amongst the wedding announcements was a photograph of Mr Thomas Stone and his new bride. It was the lady who had bought the table! Apparently she was the widow of Major Samuel Bolton of Bolton Hall, a local weathly landowner who had died earlier that year.
Of course! She remembered her now, it had been in the papers at the time, her husband suddenly died abroad and left her a small fortune, it had caused quite a stir in the town. The photograph showed the smiling couple in the main dining room of what appeared to be a large country house. They were about to cut the wedding cake but what made her peer even closer was that the cake stood on a very elaborately carved refectory table. How strange that he should get his table back and a new wife!
She wished them every happiness for the future.

About seven months later, one Thursday when the shop was closed, Miss Campbell decided to drive to the next town to shop for a new hat. She had been invited to a niece's wedding and one glance at her wardrobe told her she had nothing suitable.
As she was walking down a narrow side street she passed an antiques shop and stopped in her tracks. There, in all its glory, was the refectory table which had belonged to Tom Stone! She recognised it immediately because of its distinctive carving, she felt sure there could not be two the same. She pushed the door open and went inside for a closer look. It was still as grand as ever and she wondered what had prompted him to sell it again so soon. The assistant smiled and complimented her on her good

taste, yes, it was a handsome piece, wasn't it? He had only received it that morning from a local widower.

Her ears pricked up, did he say widower?

Yes, most unfortunate, the man had only been married a short while when his new bride - a very wealthy woman by the way – had tripped on a loose rug and hit her head against the table. She had been dead when the ambulance arrived.

With sudden foreboding Miss Campbell bent down to examine the table leg, trembling slightly. Sure enough, there were now four notches visible. She shivered involuntarily, a silent scream welling up in her throat.

She barely heard the man as he told her the previous owner would be only too pleased to meet any prospective buyer who might be interested in the tables history, he had the name and address somewhere, and he rummaged in a drawer searching for the scrap of paper.

With a cry of triumph he held it aloft only to face an empty shop, the door swinging wildly on its hinges and the bizarre sight of May Campbell running full pelt down the street as if the devil himself were after her.

Gloria Hobson

The Dead of Night

3.00am, the hour when people sleep most deeply, sometimes called the dead of night, the time when all honest folk are tucked up in bed, the time that Danny liked best.

His skinny frame almost lost in the shadows, he shuffled down The Avenue, his pinched features deep in concentration, glancing shiftily from left to right, on the look out for lights, twitching curtains, dogs barking. He needn't have worried, there wasn't a sound as the house he was seeking loomed up on his right, No. 17, the one the local kids all steered clear of.

He could understand why, the large wrought iron gates were rusty with neglect, the gardens badly overgrown and the house itself was bleak and forbidding. It seemed to look down at him with utter menace and an involuntary shiver ran down his spine. He hesitated for a moment then grinned to himself. 'Stupid fool,' he thought, 'bin reading too many of them cheap 'orror books from the market, call yerself an ex para, gerra grip man!' and he slipped quietly through the gate, making his way quickly towards the back door of the house.

His trained eye noticed a small window slightly ajar and, not for for the first time, he was thankful he had been the runt of the litter. With one last glance behind him he leapt nimbly on to the sill and squeezed through the window, lowering himself silently into the room below.

Danny stood for a moment to let his eyes get accustomed to the dark, listening intently for any sound. There was none. He moved across the room and opened a door which led into the hallway. Feeling his way cautiously along his hand came to another door. Hoping this was the main room he turned the handle with care and it opened slowly. There was a faint glow from a nearby street lamp and he looked around. All the furniture seemed very old fashioned and the carpet felt threadbare under his feet. To his disappointment there didn't appear to be a TV, stereo or computor, must be an old recluse he reckoned. But old people often kept cash at home, they didn't like banks. He cheered up at the thought.

He turned back towards the door and his heart almost stopped. In a shabby old armchair sat the figure of an old man staring balefully at him. There was a slight musty smell emanating from him and with dreadful foreboding Danny moved closer. The old mans face was a sickly grey pallor and his open mouth showed only blackened stumps. His arms hung limply over his bony knees , Danny tentatively touched his wrist, it was icy cold and there was no pulse. He must have been dead for a while.

His first instinct was to run for it, to get as far away as possible but his practical side took over. There must be something of value here and at least he could search around without being disturbed. He noticed a bureau in the corner but it was locked, where could the key be? Perhaps the old man had it on him but he was reluctant to touch him again. Screwing up all his courage (after all, the dead cannot hurt you can they?) he felt in his pockets. Nothing. He would try upstairs

The first bedroom he entered was completely empty but the second was the one he was looking for. The bed was ruffled, there were pyjamas on the floor and an open book on the nightstand. There was also a bunch of keys on a hook over the bed.

Elated, Danny grasped it and ran quickly back downstairs into the living room. As he entered he stopped in his tracks. The chair was empty.

Suddenly he heard breathing behind him, short and rasping and he could smell the musty aroma he had noticed before. The hairs stood up on the back of his scrawny neck and he felt a warm wetness in his groin as his bladder let go. His heart was pounding so heavily he felt it would explode.

He couldn't move, he was rigid with fear and then he heard shuffling as the man moved closer, clamping a cold bony hand on his shoulder. A long sharp talon gently stroked his neck where a large vein throbbed. As Danny looked up he noticed a large stained mirror on the opposite wall, the creature behind him had eyes as black as coals and when he opened his mouth, instead of the blackened stumps he had seen earlier, he saw two long white fangs moving towards his neck.

Gloria Hobson

He tried to scream but no sound came. He knew death was inevitable and he embraced it resignedly wishing only for a second that he had led a better life.

As the bright arterial blood spurted out in a gush, the old man drank his fill and Danny Morgan, ex para, ex husband, ex thief slipped silently into oblivion.

Fit For a King

It was the harshest winter anyone from the village could remember and this in countryside 300 miles east of Moscow where temperatures often dropped to minus 25 degrees. For the past six weeks it had dropped steadily and today was the lowest so far, minus 30 degrees. Snow had fallen incessantly since late October and some of the drifts were 12 feet deep making the small track to the next hamlet all but impassable.

The nearby river had been frozen for quite some time and the thick ice of the local well had to be broken with a pickaxe every morning. There was hardly any wildlife left to hunt, any crops had frozen and rotted away, food put by for the winter was fast diminishing but worst of all, the howls of the wolves from the nearby forest kept many a villager awake at night – there was nothing more frightening or dangerous than a hungry wolf.

Then came the first deaths; an elderly couple were found at the edge of the forest surrounded by bundles of firewood they had been collecting. The old woman had a broken leg and it looked as though her husband may have been trying to carry her home when he also collapsed. The ground was too hard to bury them so they were moved to an empty barn nearby, covered in sacking and left until the Spring thaw.

No one ventured out except to collect wood for the fire and water from the well. Bundled up in jumpers, coats, shawls, blankets, anything they could find, with gloves,hats and boots, it was impossible to tell men from women, children from adults. But, get close enough, look at the pinched faces and sunken eyes and it was easy to see starvation was rife.

At night, while the wolves howled and the wind whistled through the tall pine trees, death settled on the village like a mantel. Whole families slept together huddled round the tiny stove, children cried and mothers sobbed while men prayed to any gods that would listen, to end this misery. All except one that is.

The Babushka who lived in the last cottage before the forest, where the path forked, had a bright lantern burning all day and night and smoke curling from her chimney. Peope who passed could see her rosy cheeks and bright button eyes, many were afraid and crossed themselves, some called her a witch.
She must have signed a pact with the devil many thought, to still be looking so healthy and well fed.

Of course she was well aware of the gossip and the covert glances, she saw the fear and hatred in their eyes but they would soon change their minds when they wanted her help; coughs that wouldn't clear, cuts that wouldn't heal, aches, pains, agues and cramps, she had potions for them all. Not to mention the local women who needed help to get rid of certain 'encumbrances' when the last thing they needed was another mouth to feed. And the 12 year old girl raped by a boy from the next village whose parents couldn't stand the shame and wanted her help to 'solve' the problem. Ah yes, they would need her then she thought, smiling thinly through rotting teeth.

Sergei too knew of the old woman. He was 10 years old and lived with his sister, Olga 6 and Raisa 4 and his drunken father, Dimitri. Amongst the poor villagers, they were the poorest. It wasn't always so, before his mother died 2 years ago they were happy and prosperous, they had chickens in the yard and 2 goats to give milk and cheese, a fertile vegetable patch, life was sweet.

Mother was heavy with child, the village women were busy knitting and sewing for the new arrival when suddenly she awoke one morning bleeding heavily, the baby was lost and within 24 hours she too was dead. Dimitri sought solace in the vodka bottle and the children were left to fend for themselves. And now this harshest of winters was almost too much to bear.

Sergei did his best, scavenging for food, dead birds frozen in mid flight, the odd rotting vegetable – all went into the pot to make a thin rancid soup. His thoughts turned to the Babushka. That morning as he passed her cottage carrying some firewood for the stove, she was about to close her door when he caught the tantalising aroma of meat cooking, his mouth watered at the memory of it, surely she wouldn't refuse him a bowlfull for his sisters?

The girls were asleep and father was snoring loudly on the mattress in the corner. Sergei quickly put on his extra coat and stepped out into the snow. It showed no sign of abating, he looked up at the heavy, leaden sky and the cold hit him like sledgehammer, he could feel his eyelashes icing up. In a few minutes he was at her door and he knocked timidly – no reply. He knocked again, a little harder this time. Still no reply.

He tried the door which opened with a loud creak and he peered in nervously. 'Hello' he called.' Then his attention was caught by a bubbling noise and the wonderful sight of a large cooking pot over the open fire. He stepped closer and lifted the lid cautiously. The smell was overwhelming, he could see large chunks of meat, potatoes, onions and herbs, it was so wonderful he felt faint. Taking a ladel he scooped the rich mixture from the bottom of the pot and, blowing on it gently, popped some meat into his mouth, it was so tender it almost melted and he was about to try another spoonful when he heard a shuffling noise outside. She was back!

He looked around in a panic, in a one room cottage there was nowhere to hide. Then he saw a trapdoor in the corner, it must be the earth cellar where things were stored to keep cool in the summer.
As quietly and quickly as he could he lifted the trapdoor and lowered himself down. The earthen floor was frozen hard, wooden shelves lined the sides, towards the back were some sacks covered in straw, probably containing potatoes and onions, he thought. Sergei could hear footsteps above and he held his breath, if she opened the trapdoor she would surely see him but then he heard the rythmic creak of a rocking chair and breathed a sigh of relief.

Peering around he saw a small door on the back wall, this would lead outside he was sure and he edged quietly towards it. As he passed shelves he could see they were full of storage jars of various sizes, some contained stewed fruit and he was about to take one for his sisters when one of the larger jars caught his eye. The light was very dim and he peered closely his nose almost on the glass and as his eyes focused, he reeled back in horror, almost falling over in his terror.

His one aim was to get out and, in his fright, his foot caught in some sacking and he lurched against a shelf, the large jar overturning and spilling its contents all over him. A silent scream escaped his cracked lips and a sickly aroma assaulted his nostrils. Scrabbling upright he made for the door praying that it wouldn't be locked.

He pushed against it and to his relief it opened, the icy wind almost sucking the air out of his lungs as he stepped outside. Without a backward glance Sergei ran as fast as he could back to the safety of his own home.

The girls awoke as he entered, shivering at the cold draught.

'Where have you been?' asked Olga.

There was no reply.

'Have you brought us something to eat?' asked Raisa.

Sergei couldn't speak, he sat down next to the stove and gathered the girls next to him. He rocked backwards and forwards, trembling slightly and large silent tears coursed down his cheeks.

'Go back to sleep girls,' he whispered, 'I know where I can find some food tomorrow.'

He was thinking of the empty barn he had passed on his flight home. As he drifted off to sleep he imagined that, although it may not be as tasty as the unborn babies, with some garlic and a few herbs the old folk would make a meal fit for a King.

The Demon

The Demon stood on the hill overlooking the small market town and gazed down in satisfaction. He could make out the shops in the center and the deserted market-place, all in darkness now. The nearby houses, mostly respectable looking semis with neat gardens on tree-lined avenues, had a few lights on. The occasional car passed by.

A man walking his dog came towards him and murmured good night as he drew level. Melmoth, for that was his name, nodded in response. The dog whined pitifully his eyes bulging with fear as he pulled frantically on his lead.

'He knows,' thought the Demon, 'animals always do,' and his red eyes glowed slightly as he slipped away into the shadows.

Half a mile away 10 year old Charlie awoke screaming in terror from the worst dream he could remember. His mother ran into his room and scooped him up into her arms, his trembling form clinging to her, tears streaming down his cheeks. After a few minutes his shaking eased and he lay back down.

'It was awful Mom, there was this creature with red eyes and strange feet coming down the avenue towards me and I just couldn't get away …..'

His mother interrupted. 'I've told you Charlie, reading those horror books will give you bad dreams, now try to get back to sleep or you'll be too tired for school in the morning.' She turned out the light and closed the door quietly.

Charlie lay there for a few seconds, then reached out and put his bedside light back on, no way was he going to lay there in the dark. Reaching under his bed he pulled out some of the books his mother so disapproved of and began flicking through them.

As he turned the pages at random, his heart lurched. There it was! The same creature! He read carefully:

Melmoth is a Demon sent directly from Satan, set to wander the Earth for victims he can exchange forms with, thus set himself free from his bondage.

The illustration showed a figure, half man, half goat with red eyes, a dark face and cloven hooves for feet. Exactly as in his dream, Charlie shuddered, perhaps his mother was right, perhaps it was his vivid imagination that caused his nightmare. There weren't really such things as Satan and Demons were there? With this thought going round in his head, he drifted off to sleep and the book slipped out of his hand, tumbling to the floor with the red-eyed Demon grinning up at him.

Melmoth gazed down at the sleeping boy, blond hair, freckles, young and healthy, all his life in front of him. He hovered over him thoughtfully as Charlie's eyes moved rapidly under closed lids. He was dreaming of course, this would be the optimum time for the transference - Melmoth steadied himself.

Charlie's dream was the same one as before but somehow seemed more real. The Demon was standing over him and, try as he may, he could not move. It was as though an invisible force held him down and his limbs felt like lead. He tried to wake up but even that was impossible, he tossed and turned and moaned softly

Suddenly, he felt a tugging sensation and his whole body convulsed as the wrenching feeling grew stronger, it was as if his insides were being torn out. The pain was worse than anything he had ever experienced and then when he thought he must surely die, incredibly it was gone and he was enveloped by a wonderful calm. He seemed to be floating peacefully and as he looked down he could see a young boy sleeping peacefully, a boy that looked all too familiar. His heart pounding he turned towards the window where he could see his own reflection - then all became blackness.

'Come on Charlie, it's almost 7.30, you're going to be late for school,' called his mother, as she climbed the stairs wearily. She opened his door and could just make out his body shape under the covers and a tuft of hair on the pillow.

She shook him roughly and was answered by a grunt, she pulled the sheet back and Charlie blinked against the harsh light. He swung his feet out of bed and looked up at his mother.

Her screams echoed throughout the house and down the avenue at the sight of her son's brilliant red eyes and cloven hooves. Mercifully insanity overtook her as she passed out.

'Why Mummy, whatever is the matter?' Charlie croaked,' you look like you've seen a demon.'

Gloria Hobson

Can It Be Magic?

Do you believe in magic? - No?
Do you think it is all trickery and illusion? - Yes?
Well, so did I, once upon a time, but now, well let me tell you my story, see what you think ……..

Ten years ago when I was 19, I decided to take the obligatory gap year before going off to university. My older sister Alice had married an American called Ted and had gone to live near a town called Bel Harbour in Maine on the east coast. I thought I would stay there for a few weeks then travel up to Canada and maybe hitch across to Vancouver.
They had two beautiful children, Maisie aged 5 and Arnie aged 3 and one of those really wonderful clapperboard houses with a front porch looking out to sea, they were really living the American dream and I settled in straight away.

Two weeks after I arrived it was Arnie's 4th birthday and a party had been arranged. It was late August and already the autumn colours had begun to show their spectacular reds and golds. A large awning had been set up on the front lawn and a barbeque was being manned by Ted, a big jovial guy who taught science at the local High School.
As the neighbourhood kids and their parents began arriving I noticed a small pick up truck pulling into the drive. Mr Montezuma's Magic Mannikin was hand written on the side. This must be the magician they had told me about.

It was a wonderful afternoon, quite warm with a beautiful clear blue sky, with just a hint of the colder weather to come, for winters were very harsh in Maine

Excitement mounted as Mr Montezuma set out his equipment and the show began. At first it was just the usual rabbit out of a hat, silk scarves out of his sleeve and a beautiful dove which appeared out of a burst baloon. But then came his *piece de resistance* as he wheeled out a large wooden box with a door. He opened it with a flourish and, sitting inside was a life sized dummy dressed like a clown with a big red nose.

'Repeat after me children,' he called, 'Abracadabra, a doe eyed deer, please make Manni disappear', he closed the door and tapped the box with his magic wand. A sudden puff of smoke and the door sprang open. Mr Manni had gone and the children shrieked with delight.

'Shall we call him back? Mr M. asked.

'Yes!' was the excited reply.

He closed the door again. 'Repeat after me, abracadabra, a gallon of beer, please make Manni re-appear.' He tapped the box again as all the kids repeated his words, laughing loudly.

Another puff of smoke and sure enough, there was Mr. Manni the clown. Everyone applauded.

'Would any of you children like to try it ?' he asked and a few hands went up but Arnie jumped up first.

'It's my birthday,' he pleaded.

'Sure son, hop in.' Arnie squeezed in beside Manni and the door was closed. The magic words were shouted by everyone and when the door was opened, the box was empty.

It was round about now that I first felt slightly uncomfortable, just a niggling feeling in the pit of my stomach. I caught my sister's eye and she had the same look on her face. It was silly, I know, but it just didn't seem right.

However, the children all heartily called out 'Abracadabra, a gallon of beer, please make Arnie reappear' and sure enough, there they both were. I moved to pick Arnie up and he suddenly felt very cold. 'Where did you go? I asked

'Nowhere' he replied. 'I could see you all the time.'

Everyone trooped onto the porch for something to eat and I went back over to the box. I went all around it, I looked underneath searching for a trap door – nothing , no mirrors , just Mr Manni sitting looking at me. 'Where did you go?' I asked. No reply of course.

I turned and almost bumped into Mr Montezuma.

'Can I help you?' he asked, smiling thinly.

'I just wondered how the trick worked.' I mumbled sheepishly.

'No trick,' he replied. 'Just magic.' And he started to pack up his equipment.

The next day Arnie wasn't well, he'd probably got over-excited or maybe over-ate the day before, but he was running quite a temperature so my sister called the local doctor. He just said to keep him in bed for a day or two and sure enough, by the following weekend he seemed to be his usual self. I say seemed but he was just a little bit quieter than usual.

I came across him sitting on the porch hugging an old teddy. He seemed a little sad so I sat beside him and put my arm around him. 'You know when you were in the magic box' I asked? 'Could you really still see us all the time you were in there?'

'Well, all except for Maisie, there was a gap where she should have been but she was back there when I came back out ' he replied.

I thought back, I was sure Maisie hadn't moved during the show but perhaps I was mistaken.

'Everything was the same, yet it wasn't,' Arnie added. 'It was like looking in a mirror.' He started to cry. 'I'm frightened' he sobbed, 'frightened that someting bad is going to happen to Maisie.'

I tried to comfort him as best I could and eventually he fall asleep against me.

I felt quite uneasy and wondered if I should tell my sister but I didn't want to alarm her over what was probably childish imagination.

And then, tragically, a few days later, events overtook us.

The children were at nursery and I was helping my sister around the house when there was a knock at the door. Two police officers stood there looking sombre and I knew instantly it was bad news. I called to Alice and the news was broken to us that there had been an accident in the school yard and Maisie had been taken to the Emergency Room at the local hospital.

By the time we got there, it was too late, she had broken her neck falling from a swing and could not be saved.

The next few days were a nightmare that I hope I never have to go through again, no one seemed to know exactly what had happened, she was found on the ground in the playground and it was treated as a tragic accident. There were no witnesses.

The local minister, friends, neighbors, police, there were people calling all the time and then, one evening, a few days before the funeral there was another knock at the door and I went to answer it. To my surprise it was Mr Montezuma, the magician.

Can I help you?' I said.

'The question is, can I help you?' he replied enigmatically. 'Can we speak in private?'

So we sat on the porch in the near-dark.

'I heard about the little girl,' he began. 'You have my sympathy.'

'Thankyou,' I said.

'You must be going through hell.'

I didn't answer.

'You know, I may be able to help you,' he continued, 'magic isn't just about pulling rabbits out of hats, we can do a lot more than that.' He paused and looked at me as if to guage my reaction. I was intrigued but a little uneasy.

'There are …..' he paused, ' some 'rituals' shall we say that can help in a situation like this.'

'Just cut to the chase, will you,' I snapped impatiently, 'it's getting cold and supper will be ready soon.'

'Yes, sorry, well, as well as being a magician, I am also a Spiritualist, quite a good one actually. I can contact your niece but it should be done as soon after death as possible. Sometimes they can manifest themselves and -'

'Enough!' I yelled, making him jump. 'I don't want to hear any more.' I stood up. 'Please leave now, don't you realise we are distressed enough without listening to this nonsense?'

'But I only want to help, surely your sister would like to see her daughter one last time?'

'No, my niece is dead and please do NOT try to contact my sister, she is on medication and only just managing to cope. Now please go.' and I held the screen door open for him.

He went down the steps and out to his truck. I stood and watched as he drove slowly down the drive and onto the dirt road leading to the highway.

Good riddance, I thought, and went back inside shivering slightly.

That night as I lay in bed, my thoughts turned to that visit. What if he really could contact the dead? Bring Maisie back for one last time, how wonderful that would be for my sister to be able to say a last goodbye and tell her how much she was loved by everyone. But it was silly, of course, he may have meant well but it was all fantasy, just preying on the grief of the bereaved. No doubt he would demand a fee. No, some things are best left alone. With that thought, I drifted off to sleep.

The day of the funeral arrived. As you can imagine, we were all distraught and, even though my sister had been sedated she was still almost hysterical with grief. She had to be held back at the graveside, it was all too much to bear and we all returned to the house in tears. Alice went straight to her room and I followed her with a cup of tea.

'Oh, Sally, what am I to do' she cried. 'I miss her so much, if only I could have got there before she died, held her hand, told her how much we all loved her. I would do anything for that.' She sipped her tea between sobs.

I thought hard, then made my decision. I spoke to my sister and then I rang Mr Montezuma and he arranged to call the next day.

Promptly at 11.00 the next morning, when everyone was out, there was a knock on the door and I invited Mr Montezuma into the front room overlooking the Bay. I sat with Alice and held her hand while he assembled his 'magic' box with Mr. Manni in his usual place.

'Does he have to be here?' I asked.

'Oh yes' he replied, 'he is the guide you see, the go-between you might say, the link between this world and the next'.

I shivered involuntarily, wondering if I had done the right thing.

'Now, have you got something that belonged to the child, some clothing or a favourite toy maybe?' he asked.

Alice went upstairs and I took the opportunity to question him.

'Is this safe?' I asked.

'What do you mean?' he queried.

'Well, I don't want my sister to be upset any further if this doesn't work out.'

'Oh, it will, don't worry.'

Alice returned with a rag doll . 'This is her favourite,' she said, handing it over.

He placed it in the box next to Manni. 'Now Manni, I want you to go to the Dark Place, search for the child called Maisie and bring her back here. Take the doll.' He closed the door and tapped it with his wand. There was a puff of smoke and the door sprang open.

Manni and the doll had disappeared.

'Good, now all we have to do is wait,' he said, and he closed the door again, 'It wont be too long.'

We sat in silence, I could feel my sister's body getting tense, her nails digging into my hand. The room darkened and I could hear distant thunder as rain started to patter against the window. I shivered and pulled my cardigan around me tightly.

Then I heard a faint rustle and we all looked towards the box, I could feel the hairs standing up on the back of my neck and my heart began to beat rapidly.

Mr. M approached the box and tapped it with his wand. The door sprang open and a sudden flash of lightening lit up the scene. I gasped and my sister screamed involuntarily.

There sat Manni with his stupid grin.

Next to him sat Maisie, but it wasn't Maisie, not as I knew her anyway. She had on her best dress, the one she was buried in and blue ribbons in her hair, but the golden curls were dirty and a smell of decay permeated the room. She tried to smile but her face seemed to slip to one side, her head bent over at an impossible angle where her neck had been broken.

'Mummy,' she croaked.

Alice sat paralyzed, speechless with horror at this travesty of her much loved daughter. Maisie held out her hand towards her mother, the long nails caked with mud.

'I'm frightened, I don't like it here.'

'She can't stay for long,' whispered Mr. M. 'The spirits will call her back soon, if you want to say something, do it now.'

'I love you Maisie, Daddy and Arnie all send their love.' My sister said in a shaky voice. 'We're all sad you had to leave us but it will be allright, don't be afraid.' Tears rolled down her cheeks.

Suddenly, the image seemed to shimmer and grow faint, there was a sudden flash and she was gone. I blinked, had I imagined it? I walked towards the box and picked up the rag doll and I could smell the rank aroma of damp soil. A small dirty handprint was visible. I gave it to Alice, she hugged it to her, rocking backwards and forwards.

Mr. M. began to pack his equipment away quietly and I showed him to the door. He refused any payment as I shook his hand.

'I hope this has helped,' he said as he walked towards his pick up truck.

Well, did it help I asked myself? It left many more questions than answers.

It took my poor sister and her husband (she never told him about Mr. M's visit) a long time to get back to normal, I don't think life will ever be quite the same again for them, despite a new baby, Logan.

As for me, I never did get to Canada, I enrolled at a local college, met and married a local guy and settled in Bangor and gave birth to twins 2 years later. It will be their birthday soon and we are having a party.

But one thing is for sure; Mr. Montezumas Magic Mannikin will NOT be providing the entertainment.

The Eye of the Beholder

Vincent Warner had been an undertaker's assistant for about six months and, if asked, he could honestly say it was the best job he had ever had. It was tailor made for him, 'just perfic' as that guy on the telly would say.

He was, by nature, a quiet, somewhat shy young man and working down in the basement preparing bodies for funerals suited him very well. He didn't have to make small talk with others, it was peaceful and best of all, the clients couldn't answer back.

And he was good at his job, even the Boss said so, he took a fierce pride in his work and he particularly liked the re-constructive work that was sometimes required to make trauma victims look presentable for family viewing.

But it did have some drawbacks. When he tried to socialise and people asked him what he did for a living, instead of being fascinated by his job, they often turned away with a gasp of horror. Even if he invented some other proffesion people didn't warm to him, especially girls. Something about him seemed to put people off. His shy demeanor meant he had never had a proper girlfriend.

But then it happened, suddenly, unexpectedly, out of the blue, he met the woman of his dreams. She was slim, pretty, with long chestnut hair and green eyes. The minute he saw her he fell hopelessly in love and he could tell she was the one for him. Unfortunately, he could also tell that she was dead, very dead.

Gloria Hobson

She lay on the table in front of him, a suicide they said, not a mark on her beautiful face, skin like alabaster. He glanced at the chart – 22 years old, found in bed by her parents, death due to an overdose, note nearby, body to be kept pending police enquiries.

He sighed, held her hand, freezing cold of course but he locked his fingers with hers until he felt some warmth seep into her. Her lips were slightly blue so he reached for the cosmetics box he kept nearby. Selecting a bright, pink lipstick he applied it expertly, a little blusher to her cheeks brought her back to life, so to speak. He brushed her hair tenderly and arranged it around her face. He kissed her gently.

Suddenly, her eyes opened and looked into his. He stepped back startled.

'Hello,' she said softly, 'who are you?'

'Vincent,' he replied, 'what's your name?'

'Sasha. I killed myself you know.'

'Yes, I know, why did you do it?' he asked.

'Boyfriend trouble, you know what it's like. It was spur of the moment really. I wish I hadn't done it now, but it can't be undone, can it?'

'I'm afraid not,' he said, 'when you're dead, you're dead, I'm afraid.'

She sat up slowly, wincing slightly, the white sheet falling away to reveal what would have been a beautiful body had it not been for the ugly autopsy stitches. She looked down at herself and grimaced.

'Ugh, how ugly, can't you do anything about these?' she asked.

'Not really, but no one will see them 'cos you'll have a nice lacy shroud on, or your family might like to have you dressed in one of you favourite dresses if you prefer.'

'Hm, I'll have to give that some thought. I suppose Mummy and Daddy are upset, I wish I could say sorry, I really didn't mean to do it.' she sobbed quietly and Vincent put his arm around her, rocking her gently.

Suddenly, he heard footsteps coming down the stairs and he lay her down gently, covering her just as the door opened and his Boss walked in.

'Hello, talking to yourself again Vince?' he smiled, 'first sign of madness you know, you won't get much conversation out of her,' and he nodded towards the body on the table.

Vincent said nothing and busied himself preparing the embalming fluid.

'What's she like?' asked Mr Morse, peeking under the sheet, 'Oh, I see you've made a start, very good.' He collected some paperwork and opened the door.

He turned. 'Oh, by the way,' he said over his shoulder, 'the funeral can go ahead, it's set for Friday.' and he disappeared upstairs.

Sasha sat up quickly. 'Friday!' she said, 'that's only three days away.'

Vincent looked at her sadly. 'I know, it doesn't give us much time.'

'Time for what?' she asked suspiciously.

He blushed. 'I thought maybe you could be my girlfriend for a few days,' he mumbled. 'You're so very pretty.'

'But, I'm dead,' she cried 'Are you mad?' Feeling regret at her outburst she said softly, 'am I to be buried or cremated?'

He looked at his clipboard. 'Buried' he said tersly, 'with a nice oak coffin,' he added.

'But that would be awful, I don't think I could stand that, I'm claustrophobic'

'You wont be there,' he explained. 'You should have passed on by then, at the moment you are in limbo, that's what happens when you die suddenly and unexpectedly. What does it feel like, being dead, I mean?'

'Well, it's hard to describe, it's like being in a dream, a bit like walking through treacle. I want to get up and go home, but I can't move, it's very strange.' She grasped Vincent's hand.

'I'm sorry for what I said earlier, yes, of course you can be my boyfriend, it's only for a few days and I won't be as frightened if you are with me.' She thought for a moment.' 'Of course, there is one way we can be together for ever.' She looked at him shyly. 'You can come with me, we can go together, we can be soul mates if you like.'

'Oh, I don't think I could kill myself.'

'I suppose your family will miss you, your parents and so on.'

'Not really, I was orphaned as a child, as far as I know I have no relatives. I live alone and I don't have any friends.' He hesitated. 'It might not be such a bad idea after all. Let me think about it tonight.'

Next morning he arrived for work early, the building was deserted. Sasha was still on the table where he had left her, he lifted the shroud. She was as cold as ice, like a beautiful statue. Vincent stroked her cheek gently but there was no response, he opened her eyes – nothing.

'Sasha' he called gently, 'It's me, please speak to me.' But there was no response, even the dead wanted nothing to do with him, he gazed at her beautiful face and knew what he must do. He turned to the workbench and began his prearations. After 20 minutes, he was ready.

He lay alongside her on the table and attached a catheter to his arm finding a vein with ease. Turning the tap he watched as his blood began to drip into the large glass container on the floor. Satisfied that everything was in order, he slipped his arm under Sasha and held her close, her hair brushing against his cheek. His heartbeat slowed and he began to feel faint. As he kissed her cheek he thought he could hear some light breaths coming from her and suddenly she opened her green eyes and gazed at him tenderley.

'Thankyou,' she whispered and the last image before he slipped into oblivion was of her radiant smile.

'Well,' said Mr. Morse to the Police Inspector, 'I always thought he was a bit odd, obssesive you might say. He did his job well enough but he kept himself to himself, a strange boy.'

'Looks like he must have had a complete breakdown,' replied the Inspector, 'mad as a hatter if you ask me.'

They surveyed the scene in front of them.

The two corpses lay side by side, Vincent was utterly white but it was the girl who really caught their attention.

'I could understand it if she was nice looking,' said the policemen, 'but she had been dead for about a month in that tiny flat in the middle of summer before her parents found her.'

'I think she was very pretty according to photos I've seen, but decomposition had put paid to that.' said Mr Morse. 'Skin completely blackened, full of maggots, one eye missing.' He glanced at the Inspector. 'Sorry, didn't mean to upset you, I forgot not everyone is used to such things.'

'It must be true what they say, *beauty is indeed in the eye of the beholder.*' said Inspector Grayson, heading quickly for the exit.

A Holiday Tale

Many years ago when I was a child, my parents hired a small cottage in deepest Dorset for our annual holiday. It was two weeks of utter bliss, the weather was beautiful and the countryside seemed magical to a townie like me. We were about 20 miles from the coast and I enjoyed many happy hours on the sands, I particularly liked the small coves, rock pools and old smugglers caves where I could pretend to be a character in the Famous Five books I liked to read so much in the fifties.

I was as brown as a berry in no time.

The village we were on the edge of had only 10 houses, a Post Office cum general store and a large farm. It was very peaceful except first thing in the morning when the resident cockerell liked to wake us all up at the crack of dawn!

On the Tuesday we decided to drive out to a nearby ruined castle just a few miles away. The lanes were very narrow with high hedges and trees that almost touched overhead and we prayed nothing would come the other way as passing was almost impossible.

As we rounded a bend we could see the castle in the distance so we pulled onto the grass verge so my father could take some photographs. I got out with my mother and leaned against a wall to admire the view through the trees, the main tower was almost intact against a brilliant blue sky and we could see the village itself clustered around the bottom of the rise.

Suddenly I heard the rattle of wooden wheels and I looked round to see the most beautiful romany caravan I had ever seen. It was very colourfully decorated with elaborate carvings and it was pulled by a huge grey horse. An old lady held the reins and she slowed down, smiling.

'Good morning,' she croaked to my mother with a strong Dorset accent.

My mother smiled cautiously (she was never too happy around gypsies, though they always seemed very nice to me).

The old lady tapped her clay pipe against the wooden footrest and said, 'this is my usual atchers tan
(resting place), would the lady like to see some lace inside my vardo (caravan)? It's all handmade by myself, t'wd make a nice memento of your holiday.'

'Perhaps I could get something for your grandma,' said mother. 'Come along, we'll have a look.'

So we went to the back of the caravan and the gypsy lady (who told us her name was Nixi) pulled a curtain back to reveal a display of beautiful lace handkerchiefs, table cloths etc.. While my mother examined them I turned to look at the very intricate paintings on the side of the caravan; there were many strange symbols but one in particular caught my attention. It was a huge eye in brilliant colours and it seemed to stare straight at me. I ran my finger around it, following the lines carefully.

Suddenly, the curtains were flung back and the old woman called out, 'did you touch that eye, Chavo
(child)?'

'N,No,' I lied, stammering nervously.

' Please don't my dear, it's bad luck for me if Gorgios (non gypsys) touch it,' and she disappeared back inside. I looked after her feeling a bit guilty.

Chastised, I went to look at the horse instead, stroking him gently, the name on his collar was Wester.

Then my mother appeared suddenly, holding a very pretty shawl.

'Your grandma will love this, it's so beautifull,' she said, obviously very pleased with her purchase.

We said goodbye and went back to the car where my father was waiting patiently. We pulled away and headed towards the castle, Nixi staring balefeully at us.

The rest of the day was spent pleasantly, we had a tour of the castle and were then left to explore at liberty. I loved old castles, I liked to imagine what it would have been like to live in them - very draughty I suppose. Then we went for lunch at the village Inn – the Black Bear. In the afternoon we called at an antiques market where my father bought an old camera to add to his collection.

Well, the week passed very pleasantly, then, on the Saturday we visited a nearby town on the coast and wandered the quayside lookng at all the boats, many from abroad, Polish, French Swedish, some small, some large. Near the Lifeboat Station we sat on a bench to eat the sandwiches mother had brought. A family sat close by with a cute puppy, he ran towards us and cheekily took a bite out of my ham teacake and we all laughed. A conversation sprang up, the usual holiday chat. My mother mentioned our encounter with the gypsy and the beautiful lace she had bought for grandma.

They seemed very interested and asked many questions about the old gypsy and her caravan.

'Have you seen the local paper?' asked the man, rummaging in his rucksack. 'Look at this,' and he handed it over. The main headline read 'GYPSY TRAGEDY - on Tuesday afternoon an old lady known locally as Nixi was killed when her caravan was in collision with a tractor on a narrow country lane near Corfe. Her horse, Jasper, had to be put down by a local vet.'

There was a picture of the wrecked caravan on its side, the EYE that had so fascinated me, was clearly visible.

'How awful,' said my mother clearly upset. 'It must have happened just after we left her, I can hardly believe it.'

I felt a sudden chill in the air, despite the warm sunshine, as I remembered what she had said about bad luck if a non-gypsy touched the eye. I never told anyone about that, of course, they would think I was mad.

I am not normally superstitious but on this occasion I did not want to tempt fate. I often wonder if I caused the accident, but I will never know for sure.

Gloria Hobson

We still have the shawl, when Grandma died, my mother inherited it and now I have it, it is in a locked suitcase in the attic. I daren't get it out as I don't want to be the next recipient of a gypsy curse.

Willows

Eion Jenkins eyed with trepidation the grim facade of the Green Willows Retirement and Nursing Home. 'It doesn't look very welcoming,' he complained to his daughter Sian as she pushed his wheelchair up the driveway towards the main door.

'All these old Victorian mansions look like this on the outside, Dad,' she replied, 'I'm sure it will look much cheerier inside, it comes highly recommended.' She pressed the doorbell.

The heavy door swung open and a pretty young girl stood smiling at them.

'Hello, you must be Mr Jenkins,' she said brightly. 'We've been expecting you, do come in.' She closed the door behind them.

The entrance hall was dimly lit and quite cool but there were fresh flowers on a table and it smelled nicely of beeswax polish.

'If you'd like to wait in the lounge, I'll get Mrs Williams, the Matron, to come and show you around.'

The lounge had a large TV in the corner, tuned to an afternoon soap, but most of the residents seemed to be dozing, a few were reading and one old lady was knitting a colourful shawl.

The door behind them opened.

'Good afternoon, I'm Mrs Williams, welcome to Green Willows.'

A stout lady stood before them wearing a dark blue, highly starched uniform.

'We'll have a quick tour and then I'll have your luggage brought in and you can settle into your room.'
She said brightly, hustling them back out into the hallway.

Within 15 minutes they were outside Room 22 on the second floor. Mrs Williams opened the door for them, hurried away to order collection of his cases. The room was quite small but very cosy. There was a telephone and television and a comfy looking armchair. Fresh linen on the bed and clean towels in the bathroom completed the picture.

'Well, Dad, I think this looks very nice, don't you?' said Sian.

'Humph' grunted Eion. 'I suppose it will have to do, I just hope the food is good.'

Sian ignored him and pushed his wheelchair into the corner as he sat in the armchair. He only needed it for long distances, could manage quite well without it for short spells.

A tap on the door and Mrs Williams popped her head round the corner. 'Tea at 3.00, evening meal at 6,' she announced. 'You're welcome to stay for tea,' she said to Sian and disappeared again.

Sian left at 4.00 after helping her father unpack and said she would visit at the weekend. 'If you want anything, sweets, books etc, just give me a ring.' And she kissed him on the cheek.

The first few days passed pleasantly enough. There was a strict routine but being X Army, Eion preferred that, you knew where you were with rules and regulations and he liked discipline. His parents had died in a fire when he was 5 and he was brought up in various foster homes, then, at 18, he had joined the Army and travelled a lot. His married life was spent in various married quarters, mostly in Germany. He also spent some time in Canada and Cyprus and finally resigned after 35 years service. A few security jobs took him up to retirement, then he was widowed and went to live with his daughter and her family near Brecon in Wales.

Then a stroke a year ago meant she could no longer look after him, so here he was. He never wanted to end his days in a home, but there was no alternative.

On the 4th day he went to bed at his usual time, 11.15, but he was awoken suddenly about an hour later by the loud creaking of the wardrobe door. It was swinging slightly on its hinges so Eion got out of bed and closed it firmly. He was just about to nod off again when the squeeking started again. This time he left the door ajar and wedged his slipper under it. 'There, that should do it' he thought as he clambered back into bed.

When he awoke next morning he reached under his bed grasping for his slippers and had put them on before he remembered the previous night. He looked across at the wardrobe, it was shut tight, but he was sure he had put one of his slippers under it to stop the squeaking.
'Must have dreamt it,' he concluded, dressing quickly and going down for breakfast.
'Are you sleeping well?' asked his neighbor at the breakfast table, introducing himself as Joe.
'Yes, not too bad.'
'Which room are you in?' asked Joe, stabbing at a piece of bacon.
'22,' replied Eion, taking a sip of his tea.
Joe's hand stopped halfway to his mouth and his eyes widened.
'Is that a problem?' asked Eion
'Well, that room has been locked for quite some time, I'm surprised it's been re-opened. I spent one night in it myself when I first came but then I asked to be moved.'
'Oh, and why was that?' queried Eion, though he thought he might know the reason.
'The wardrobe door kept me awake all night and I just didn't like the feel of the room, couldn't quite put my finger on it. Mrs Williams probably thought I was crazy.' He laughed nervously.

That night, before undressing, Eion examined the wardrobe thoroughly and inside, on a hook, he found a small key. It fit the lock perfectly. He put the key under his pillow before getting into bed and he was soon asleep.

Tap, tap, tap. Eion opened his eyes. The door was open and as his eyes adjusted to the dark he thought he could see shadowy shapes near his bed and a musky smell filtered into the room. He thought he could hear a slight whispering nearby.

He closed his eyes and tried to keep calm, not much frightened him nowadays but he could feel his heart start to pound. There was definitely someone in the room, he could hear raspy breathing.

A sudden loud bang almost made him fall out of bed and his eyes flashed open.

The room seemed completely normal, no shadows or noises, the wardrobe door was shut tight. He reached under his pillow to find the key where he had placed it earlier and he got out of bed and unlocked the wardrobe. Everything seemed to be in order

There was a sharp rap on the door. It was the Night Nurse.

'I was just passing and heard a loud bang, are you alright?' she asked.

'Yes. Fine. Just dropped a book on the floor' he explained, 'nothing to worry about.'

She left and he sat on the edge of the bed. There most definitely was something to worry about, but what? He wasn't a great believer in the supernatural, he was a very practical person. There must be a rational explanation. He finally went back to sleep and was not disturbed again

At breakfast next day Joe asked, 'you don't look too good, not getting much sleep are you?'

Eion said nothing.

'You can tell me, you know. Don't forget, I've been in that room, I've heard the tapping and squeaking, seen the shadows. I know how frightening it can be.'

'I don't know what to do,' confessed Eion, 'there must be an explanation, if I tell Mrs. Williams she'll just laugh at me. But it does seem to be getting worse, I'll soon be at the stage when I daren't go to bed.'

'Well, if things get too bad, come and get me, I'm in room 30, but personally, I would ask to be moved, people do it all the time.'

That night Eion did something he hadn't done for years; he got out an old Bible from his service days and said some half-remembered prayers before he went to bed. He kept his bedside light on and put the radio on quietly for company. He felt like a little boy again, frightened of the dark. He tried to stay awake but eventually his eyes closed.

This time it was the silence that woke him, the radio was dead and the light was off. Dark shapes circled his bed, they seemed to be calling his name softly. He got out of bed and was inexorably drawn towards the wardrobe, he tried to resist but all his strength seemed to desert him. Strong arms gripped him fiercely and propelled him across the room. Hot, fetid breath was all around him. He opened his mouth and tried to scream but he could only manage a faint croak.

'I must be dreaming,' he thought. 'Please God, let me wake up!'

The wardrobe door opened silently in front of him and Eion's knees buckled under him. It was a vision of Hell. Small creatures with red eyes danced in front of him, the wardrobe appeared to go back into infinity and flames were everywhere. The heat was unbearable and then a face materialised in front of him, a face like no other; the skin was blackened and blistered, one eye had gone and the other was weeping a hideous, smelly yellow pus. The mouth was a red slash and sharp, green looking teeth could just be seen through parted lips.

A rictus grin stretched the skin so much the face was in danger of splitting completely and two horny arms reached out to embrace him tightly.

Eion screamed as hot talons sank into him amd he could smell his own flesh burning. He was pulled into the wardrobe and the door slammed shut behind him.

When he didn't appear for breakfast the next morning, one of the assistants went to check on him. She tapped lightly on the door and when there was no reply, pushed the door open tentatively.

Eion was in bed with just the top of his head showing and she approached him nervously.

'Are you getting up today?' asked Glenys, 'You'll miss breakfast if you don't. Do you feel ill?'

No reply.

She pulled the duvet back gently and stared with horror at the sight in front of her. She ran screaming hysterically from the room and ran downstairs.

The Doctor was summoned and together with Mrs Williams, approached the bed side. The corpse was completely black and shrivelled, the sking sloughing off in places, bits of flesh sticking to the sheets. There was no sign of a fire anywhere in the room.

'Better inform the family, Mrs Williams,' said Dr. Thomas, 'though God knows what we can say for the cause of death, we'll have to leave that to the Coroner.'

'Could it be spontaneous combustion? Asked Mrs Williams.

'I have heard of that but it is very rare', replied the Doctor, 'It's highly unlikely'

They turned to go and the Doctor said, 'Oh, by the way, you might like to do something about that wardrobe door, the constant squeeking and creaking is enough to drive you insane.'

An Eye For An Eye

Ahmed hurried down the steep, rocky path leading from his home to the village below, his mother gazing anxiously after him. She always worried when he left and had begged him not to go but it was important that he had the time to do what must be done and return by nightfall.

He must get back before dark so that the door could be firmly locked, the old heavy dresser pulled across it and shutters put in place across the windows.

The cemetery was on some waste ground near the Mosque and he opened the rusty gate, the hinges screeching in protest. Many of the graves were unmarked but the one he wanted had a modest headstone. Ahmed paused in front of it listening intently but it was deathly quiet, all that could be heard were distant sounds from the village and some goats on the opposite hillside.

He knelt down and reached in his pocket for a small phial. He took the stopper off and sprinkled the contents over the mound of earth, muttering a prayer as he did so. Ahmed glanced up as some birds flew overhead and he realised it was getting darker, he must hurry.

Running up the hill he stumbled on some loose shale and he swore under his breath. The shadows were getting longer and he felt as though they were reaching out for him. As he rounded a bend he could see the tiny dwelling up ahead, his mother standing by the door.

'Hurry son' she called and Ahmed threw himself at the door which she slammed shut behind him.

Between them they tugged the ancient dresser into place and then checked all the window shutters were firmly closed. Only then could they relax and mother made some sweet tea which they sipped quietly in front of a small stove.

'This can't go on Mother' Ahmed said finally, 'it's impossible to do this every night, I haven't the energy'. He was 15 but felt like an old man.

'But he wont rest,' she protested, 'what else can we do?'

'We will have to find the man who killed him,' he replied, 'only then will he leave us alone'

Ahmed thought back to the day his father died, 2 weeks ago, just after Friday prayers.

They'd walked through the market place and Ahmed had stopped to buy some sugared almonds for his mother, while his father went on ahead. As he hurried to catch up he heard scuffling noises and a muffled cry and as he rounded a bend he saw his father leaning against a wall clutching his belly.

A large scarlet stain was spreading across his tunic and as his hands fell away he slipped quietly to the ground, the blood pooling round him.

The rest of the day was a blur. He could vaguely remember people rushing to help, his mother screaming hysterically, his father being carried away and officials from the Mosque murmering prayers over him.

As was the custom, he was buried next day. Enquiries were made but no one had heard or seen anything suspicious. As far as he knew his father had no enemies, he led a quiet life and made his living as a carpenter. No one was arrested, no motive could be found and the matter was quietely laid to rest but for Ahmed and his mother there was to be no rest for quite some time.

Just days after the funeral, late at night, there was a loud banging on the door. Armed with a heavy skillet, Ahmed approached the door cautiously, his mother close behind. Opening the door nervously they peered out into the blackness but there was no one to be seen. Holding a lantern, Ahmed went around the house and the small olive grove but there was nothing. Must be the wind they concluded.

But it happened the next night and the one after that, becoming louder each time until it seemed the whole house was shaking. On the 4th night they waited expectantly but it remained quiet, just a soft breeze that rattled the window and a scuffling noise which somehow seemed even more frightening.

Sleep was impossible and they were exhausted. They sat by the stove all night, sipping tea, blankets round their shoulders and waited for the dawn.

They discussed what to do. 'I will go and see the Imam,' said Ahmed, 'Ask his advice''

'Don't bother' said his mother, 'he will only dismiss you.'

'But the phiall is almost empty, then what can we do?'

We will slaughter another goat if we have to, only fresh blood can be used,' she said.

'But it doesn't make it stop' protested Ahmed, 'We can't continue for ever'.

'We will do what we must ' murmered his mother, ' now try and get a little sleep while I milk the goats.

Ahmed drifted off but a short time later he awoke with a start. A noise from the corner of the room caught his attention, there was a familiar looking figure on the old mattress his parents used to share.

Sitting upright, his head turned slowly towards Ahmed, hollow eyes staring balefully at his son.

Ahmed thought his heart would surely stop as he gazed in terror at his dead father – this was no dream.

The spectre arose and seemed to float towards him, a rank stench of easth and decay assaulted his nostrils. His father stood in front of him and holding out his hand dropped something on the ground. Ahmed was held in a grip of fear as his father leant towards him and tried to speak but only a croak issued from his putrefying lips.

'What do you want me to do?' cried Ahmed, his eyes bulging with dread.

There was a sound from the door as his mother entered.

'Who are you talking to?' she asked

Ahmed looked around but the ghost had disappeared and he knew she wouldn't believe him.

'I was just dreaming, 'he replied, and as his mother busied herself making tea he hastily snatched up the key from the earthen floor and slipped it into his pocket.

Later, he hurried down to the village for bread and, as he passed the cemetery he saw a heavily veiled woman near his father's grave. Hiding behind an old fig tree he watched as she laid some wild flowers on the ground and as she left through he creaking gate he decided to follow her.

She skirted the village and paused outside a heavy ornate door which she quickly unlocked. Ahmed just had a fleeting glimpse of a large courtyard and a small fountain before the door closed behind her.

After a few minutes he approached stealthily and took the key out of his pocket, it fitted easily and he slipped quietly inside. To his left a door was slightly ajar and he could hear someone sobbing quietly. Peering carefully round the corner he could see it was the same woman, this time unveiled; she was very beautiful with thick glossy hair halfway down her back.

Suddenly she twisted round and with a cry of alarm she tried to slam the door shut but Ahmed blocked it with his foot.

'What do you want?' she cried, 'I'll scream if you don't go'.

'I simply want to talk to you,' he said quietly, 'I am Ahmed, son of Rashid,'

The woman paled.

'I am trying to find out who murdered him'.

Her eyes welled and large tears rolled down her cheeks, 'I can't help you' she said at last, 'how did you get in?'

'My father gave me a key, 'Ahmed replied. She seemed surpised.

'When? she asked.

'This morning.'

Her eyes widened, then glazed over and she sank to the ground in a faint. Ahmed found a damp cloth and placed it on her forehead. After a few moments she sat up.

'Did you say this morning?' she murmured.

He nodded. 'His spirit came to me, he cannot rest until we find the person responsible, you must know something'

She stared at him for a long moment as if trying to decide how much to tell him.

Then, 'It was my husband, Khalid,' she said at last, 'he was jealous you see, your father cameto do some work here and he got this stupid idea unto his head that we were lovers.'

'And were you?'

'No, of course not!. But Khalid didn't believe me and he beat me. Your father saw my bruises and confronted him and my husband swore he would kill him if he saw him again. That day, when he came home, he was spattered with blood, he made me burn his clothes in the yard and said he would kill me too if I ever told anyone. What shall we do?'

Ahmed thought for a moment, 'Where is he now?'

'In the fields to the south, hunting for rabbits. He'll be back in about an hour'

Taking his leave, Ahmed headed to the southern edge of the village and, sure enough, in a small copse, he could see a tall man resting on a fallen tree stump. As Ahmed approached he looked up.

'Khalid?' he called.

'Yes' replied the man, 'who are you?'.

'I am Ahmed, son of Rashid,' he replied.

Khalid stood up instantly, holding his shotgun tightly.

'I want to talk to you about his death.'

'I don't know what you are talking about, I had nothing to do with it,' muttered Khalid.

'I believe you killed him and I intend to report you to the Imam and he will inform the police'.

He steppd toward Khalid who sneered and held his shotgun menacingly.

'Come any closer and I will kill you too,' Khalid called out in warning.

Ahmed took another stride forward and Khalid stepped further back. Suddenly his foot caught in a tree root and Khalid fell backwards. As he hit the ground the shotgun went off with a terrific bang that almost perforated Ahmeds' eardrums, blue smoke curled upwards and the pungent smell of cordite filled the air.

Gloria Hobson

As his head cleared Ahmed could see Khalid lying on the stoney ground, he approached carefully but it was clear he was dead. The top of his head was missing.

Ahmed hurried home, shocked at what had happened. He hadn't intended him to die, he simply wanted justice done. He called at the cemetery and knelt in front of his fathers grave. He took the key out of his pocket and buried it in the loose soil
'Rest now' he whispered, tears in his eyes.

As usual, his mother was waiting anxiously for him and she slammed the door shut behind him and started to tug at the heavy dresser. Ahmed stopped her.
'No need for that,' he told her gently, 'we wont be disturbed any more. He is at peace now.'

A Gift From Zaria

They say women are from Venus and men are from Mars. You might think, as did I, that this is just the usual trans-Atlantic psycho babble, but let me tell you it can be true. Want to hear more? Then lock the door, take the phone off the hook and find a comfy chair by the fire, then read on………..

It was about 20 years ago and I was a student at a university in the North East. I was out on my usual Sunday morning jog around the local park, it was early Spring, quite fine and pleasant.

After my second circuit around the boating lake I decided to take a rest on a nearby bench. I rested my head back and closed my eyes, I was deep in contemplation about whether to have Pot Noodles or Spaghetti Hoops for lunch (I was a penniless student after all) when I felt the movement and heard the creak of someone sitting beside me.

I looked out of the corner of my eye and could hardly believe what I saw; the most beautiful creature with long blond hair and green eyes, smiling at me. I had to pinch myself to make sure I wasn't dreaming.

' Hello,' she said, ' my name is Zaria, what's yours?'

'Hi, I'm Simon,' I replied, slightly tongue-tied for once.

'I come to seek my friend, I have not seen him for 3 days, we sometimes argue and he comes here because it is very peaceful, will you help me find him?' asked Zaria.

She had a strange accent that I couldn't quite place though her English was very good if a little stilted.

'What does your friend look like?' I asked.

'Like me,' she replied.

'Perhaps he has gone back home,' I suggested, ' have you checked?'

'Oh, no, that's not possible, the alignment is not right.'

' Alignment?' I said. 'Where do you come from?'

'Venus,' she said, 'Zanta is from Mars but we live on Venus. We like to visit Earth because it is so beautiful.

Well, herein lies the quandary, do I sidle off the bench and make a run for it or do I stay and try to humour her, she seemed so matter of fact but was obviously as mad as a hatter. Considering that Venus is more than 80 million miles from Earth, I asked the obvious question.

'How did you get here?

'Using the Quark method, of course, how else?' Tears welled up in her eyes.' We have to return in 2 days or we will dissimilate and our atoms will be scattered throughout the universe,' she sobbed quietly. 'We cannot maintain human form for very long, we are really reptilian but we can adapt according to which planet we visit, we try to blend in.'

Yeah sure, I thought*, she's been watching too many sci-fi films.*

'You do not believe me, I can tell,' she sniffed. 'You think I am crazy but I can prove it………..'

Before she could complete her sentence, her eyes widened as she focused on something over my shoulder.

I turned around to see two men approaching from the direction of the tennis courts. Behind them, by the main gate, a small ambulance was parked with its blue light flashing.

'There you are, Zaria,' the first man exclaimed, 'We've been looking for you, come on my dear, let's go back to the hospital and you can have some lunch.'

Zaria hunched back on the bench, her eyes loked at me pleadingly and I looked away in embarrassment. What could I do?'

'What about Zanta?' she asked the man.

'You know about him, we told you he had gone away, don't you remember? Come on now'

Reluctantly she stood up and with a last glance at me, went quietly back to the ambulance. I looked down because I couldn't bear to see her sad figure, it seemed such a shame that such a beautiful young girl should have such serious mental problems.

Suddenly, I heard a loud bang and then a sudden gust of wind almost blew me off my seat, I looked over towards the ambulance as a whoosh of flames shot 20 feet into the air so fiercely that no one could have possibly survived. No one could get near and by the time the Fire Brigade arrived, all that was left was a smouldering heap of twisted metal.

Of course, the story got front page headlines next day but no real explanation was ever given for the explosion, some sort of fuel leak was the general consensus.

A few days later I went back to the park, some people had put flowers near the scene, the asphalt had melted and the grass and surrounding shrubs were all scorched. Scuffing around my eye was caught by something bright among the debris. I picked it up and gave it a cursory wipe on my sleeve and then I almost dropped it with surprise. It vibrated slightly and seemed icy cold against my palm.

It was about the size of a 50 pence piece but a lot heavier, plain on one side but with a symbol on the other rather like a claw. I slipped it into my pocket and went home deep in thought.

I have it still. As I write this it is on a small table nearby, vibrating slightly, my gift from a beautiful green-eyed Venusian.

Gloria Hobson

A Night on Pendle Hill

Everyone has heard of the Pendle Witches of 1612 – Yes? Well, not everyone of course. The question is do YOU believe in witches? Nowadays, the answer would be a resounging NO! But a few centuries ago, they seemed to be in almost every village in the country. Even so-called learned scholars treated it as fact when really, I suppose, they were just poor old women with a cat for company, who knew how to collect certain herbs to heal everyday aches and pains.

A lot, of course, was envy and malicious gossip. The true test was the 'ducking stool' - The suspect person would be tied to a chair or stool, thrown into a pond or river. If they floated they were said to be a witch (the Devil was thought to imbue them with magic powers to protect them from sinking). If they sank (and presumably drowned) they were thought to be innocent! It was a 'no win' situation.

But to get back to Pendle, a small town in East Lancashire. There are plenty of books about the place and what happened is well documented. After the suspects were arrested and tried, they were executed at Lancaster Castle in 1612.

Pendle Hill itself is visible from quite a distance and there is no doubt it looks quite spooky. But, whatever you do, do not go on Halloween, it is far too crowded, better go January or February when it is quieter. A misty night is even more atmospheric.

But let me tell you about a bunch of friends who did just that. We met every Wednesday in the local pub, ostensibly for the Quiz Night and the slender chance of winning the 50 pound jackpot but really just to get as drunk as possible.

Well, one night my girlfriend Emily, whose father was a history teacher, brought some books all about Pendle and suggested that we hire a van and go and spend the weekend there.

'Perhaps we might see old 'Demdike' there.'

' Who?' someone asked.

'Read up about it, it might inspire you. It will be fun anyway,' she said.

So, it was planned. We borrowed some sleeping bags and bits and pieces, food and, of course, a few beers and arranged to meet on Friday afternoon, intending to be back sometime on Sunday.

I studied one of the books which had some quite imaginative sketches of witches on broomsticks flying through the sky against a full moon, you know the type of thing! But, putting all that to one side, it was very informative with handy maps showing the best locations.

We set off in high spirits.

Our first port of call was the Heritage Centre at Barrowford where we had a welcome drink of hot chocolate and I bought a Witchy teatowel for my Grandma.

It was getting dark as we left so we headed for St Mary's Church in New Church where Alice Nutter was supposed to be buried although this is disputed. After her execution her family spirited her body away. There is a grave with her name on it and a skull and crossbones carving. There is also an 'Evil eye' on the church turret to ward off evil spirits. People obviously took it very seriously.

We all gathered round the grave, the only sound was the squeaking of bats as they dive bombed us - I hate bats!

Our last port of call for the day was the Pendle Witch Inn at Barley where we had a pint and a ploughmans.

By now it was fully dark, there were no street lights and the roads were quite narrow. It was time to find somewhere to park up for the night.

As we rounded a bend there was a sudden bang from under us and we slewed to a halt on the grass verge, narrowly missing a tree. A quick inspection showed a very flat rear tyre, no need to panic, it shouldn't be too difficult, we were four healthy young men (and two healthy girls) I should add.

But the problem was we could not find the spare! So we decided to ring the breakdow number we had been given, the trouble was, none of our phones worked, reception can be poor out in the sticks. We would have to find a public phone the next day.

Well, as it was getting late, we thought we would settle down for the night, it was cosy enough enough with the sleeping bags and some old mattresses we had brought. A couple of beers and we were soon asleep.

The next thing I could remember was some loud thumping on the side of the van and I looked out of the rear window and was startled to see a couple looking in at us.

I explained the situation and said we were going to sort things out in the morning.

The man, whose name was Jim, said we were parked in a dangerous spot – he had almost run unto us as he came round the bend. His wife, Penny, suggested we all come to their farm which was about a mile away, and ring from there in the morning.

I would have been happy to stay where we were but the girls insisted we take the offer up – at least there would be a bathroom and a proper toilet. So we all piled into their pickup truck and sped off down the road.

A sign to the left said 'Malkin House' and a dirt road led to a neat and tidy small house half hidden among the trees. Some of the outbuildings looked in need of repair but the house itself was very cosy. In the main room a cheery fire was burning so I definitely think we made the right decision.

After a warm drink we were left to settle down on the various chairs and soon fell asleep.

I awoke with a start, I don't know what time it was or what had woken me. The I heard it, a scratching noise coming from the window nearby. It got louder so I pulled the curain back but could see nothing. Then I heard an even louder scratching at the door. Thoroughly spooked by now I nudged Emily but she just mumbled something about the cat wanting to come in out of the cold. I rolled over and, despite still feeling uneasy, I eventually went back to sleep.

The next morning, Penny came in with a plateful of bacon butties- most welcome! I was just telling everyone about the night before, to peals of laughter, when she interrupted.

'Oh, so you met old Demdike did you?

'What!' I said, 'you mean the old witch, surely not.'

'Oh yes, you aren't the first. When anyone new comes, especially at night, she tries to get their attention. She wants to come home'.

'Did you say home? What do you mean?'

'Well, this building was part of a large farm called 'MALKIN TOWERS'. It was in such a poor state when we bought it, we only decided to renovate this part. She lived here with Anne Chattox, another suspected witch. They were both executed at Lancaster Castle, of course, you've probably read about them. We've never heard Anne but old Demdike is always curious when someone new comes to the house. She seems harmless enough, just a bit scary, but we are used to her now.

Well, that's the tale, we left with plenty to think about, we got the van sorted out eventually and decided to head home early.

We agreed we would not tell anyone about our night in Malkin House, they would probably say we'd had too many beers. Maybe we had, but it all seemed very real to me.

So, if anyone ever asks me about the Pendle Witches I tell them to approach it with an open mind and if you must go, please book into a nice B & B for the night, don't try camping!

Gloria Hobson

The Dentist

John Bolton had been afraid of the dentist for as long as he could remember. He thought his phobia had probably begun when he was five and his mother had taken him with her when she needed some new dentures re-aligning.

As he sat in the cold waiting room he could hear a child screaming nearby and the awful high-pitched whine of a drill. Even when he only went for a routine inspection he broke into a cold sweat.

But one good thing came out of all this; he took excellent care of his teeth, he brushd them 3 or 4 times a day with a good quality toothpaste, flossed and gargled every night and avoided sugary food. As a result he had never had any problems. Until now that is.

John had woken up with agonising toothache and when he looked in the bathroom mirror had been horrified to see that one side of his face was badly swollen. He knew immediately what that meant, of course; an abcess. He had seen people in the waiting room looking extremely miserable as they waited for treatment. Some paracetamols eased it slightly but it soon returned with a vengeance and he knew he would have to seek help.

He had recently been promoted at the Bank and had been re-located to a town 150 miles away. He had been so busy he had not got round to registering at a new practice so he dug out the telephone directory.

There were three in his neighborhood, the first was closed on Mondays, the second could accept no new patients but the third – the P. White Dental Practice- could see him at 2.30 this afternoon.

At 2.00 clock he left his small flat to walk the half a mile to Lineham Road. As he got nearer, the old fears returned and he almost turned back but he knew he couldn't. Surely dental treatment and techniques had improved in the last 20 years, it should be pain free these days, he tried to console himself but without much success.

He walked up the steps and opened the front door, it was quite dingy and looked as though it could do with a lick of paint. He entered the door on his right marked Waiting Room, rang the bell at the counter and looked around him; dark green linoleum, black leather furniture and a stained coffee table holding old copies of National Geographic magazines. Not very welcoming.

'Can I help you?' a voice behind him made him jump.

'John Bolton, I rang this morning,' he said.

'Please take a seat.' she looked as plain and severe as the surroundings, no glamour girls here, he thought as he sat down next to a grimy window.

It was very quiet, no other patients or noises from the consulting rooms.

The nurse returned. 'Mr White will see you now,' she said holding the door open for him.

He stepped through into a nightmare.

Mr White stood behind an old-fashioned dentists chair holding the most enourmous syringe John had ever seen. He was tall and cadarverous with a stoop and a slight twist to his back. He smiled to show a set of yellow ill-fitting dentures. 'Not a good advert for his proffesion' thought John, his heart racing.

'I can't do this.' And he turned towards the door but the nurse blocked his way.

'Please sit down, Mr Bolton, no need to be nervous,' said Mr White'

As John edged himself into the chair he immediately felt a prick in his neck and almost instantly his face became cold and numb, the paralysis quickly spreading through the rest of his body, his arms and legs were completely immobile, yet he was fully conscious, his eyes wide open and his brain racing.

The nurse took his arm and quickly and efficiently attached a catheter to it. Arranging severel large glass jars on a nearby table, a narrow tube leading from his arm into the first one. An adjustment was made and immediately blood began slowly dripping into the jar.

John watched out of the corner of his eye almost hypnotically as his life blood drained away. The tube was soon moved to the next jar and he began to feel faint. The room started spinning.

After rhe 3rd jar was full, the tiny tap was turned off and he fell into a fitful sleep.

When he awoke it was dark and he seemed to be in a narrow bed with a small amount of light coming from a single weak bulb. He could hear heavy snoring coming from his left and small rustling noises coming from his right. But he couldn't move even though his numbness appeared to have worn off, then he realised to his horror, that he was held down by tight leather straps.

Turning his head, he could see a small bed on either side and three more opposite. It was dark and dirty, like a cellar, with cold stone walls. What was this place?

He could still feel the catheter in his arm and as he raised his head, he could see the other 'patients' were similarly burdened. It seemed to be some sort of blood collection service, an illegal one, of course!

It was what might happen next that alarmed him, was the blood to be sucked out of them all until they were all dried husks. And then what? It was like something out of a horror film and he knew how they usually ended.

'Hello,' he whispered, 'is anybody awake?'

Silence. He tried again.

'Can anybody hear me?'

Still nothing

Then he heard footsteps and the sound of a key turning. The door creaked open. He closed his eyes and feigned sleep. He could smell a faint antiseptic odour and hear the rustle of a skirt. It must be the nurse cometo check on her 'patients'. Her footsteps stopped at the side of his bed and she took his wrist to check his pulse. After a few minutes she left and he breathed a sigh of relief and drifted off to sleep.

The pain was excruciating, throbbing waves of agony that seared through him like daggers, anguish that made him cry our loud. The blackness lightened slightly and a tiny dot of light appeared in the centre and slowly expanded as his eyes adjusted. John opened them cautiously to a blinding whiteness.

A face loomed over him and he cringed automatically, shrinking back into the pillow. He felt a coldness creep through his veins as a hyperdermic sank into his arm.

'No more blood please, no more,' he murmured, 'please just let me die.' He screwed his eyes shut as the pain gradually subsided.

'Feeling better now, Mr Bolton?' a friendly voice asked.

John looked up. A pretty blond nurse smiled down at him.

'Where am I?' he croaked.

'St. Justins,' she replied, 'you've had a very bad infection, the abcess on you gum burst as your dentist examined you and you had to be admitted because you were hallucinating. You must have lost a lot of blood because we had to give you a transfusion but the antibiotics will soon have you right again, just try to rest and you can go home in 24 hours if the Doctor agrees.'

A week later and he was almost back to normal. He had a few days sick leave left so decided to take a walk to Lineham Road to thank the dentist.

He went up the steps and through the door and to his surprise found the place completely empty. The waiting room was bare and dusty and the consulting room had only a few old X rays on the wall and a sink with a dripping tap.

There was a door in the far corner which opened with a familiar creak. John peered down into the darkness of a cellar. Stealing himself he descended slowly using his lighter to guide him, pushing dusty cobwebs out of his way.

It was empty and he sighed with relief - it had been a dream after all!

He turned to go and something caught his eye, something glinting in the corner. He bent down and froze in horror. The broken rim of a large glass jar lay there alongside some plastic tubing.

He scrambled in panic back up the stairs and out of the main door.

Gloria Hobson

John ran down the street scattering startled pedestrians right and left. They must have thought he was crazy as they heard him muttering something about getting home *AS SOON AS POSSIBLE* because he needed to clean his teeth!!

Pitter – Patter

I first heard the pitter-patter of tiny feet early one morning as I prepared to take a shower. I had an important interview for a job and wanted to look my best. As I stood waiting for the water to heat up, it suddenly got louder and seemed to move across above my head, like a small army on a parade ground.

I looked up, don't ask me why 'cos there was nothing to be seen. What could it be? The attic was seldom used, old toys, suitcases that never came out, a box of National Geographic magazines, bits of furniture, the usual stuff.

It was a place I hardly ever visited. I didn't like the musty smell and the dust motes that floated about like snow flakes. I would try to investigate later, after my interview I had the rest of the day off.

Well, the interview came to nothing, as was often the case. The trouble was I only managed a year at University before my father had a stroke and , as I was the only family he had, I had to leave. An only child, I had some cousins in Canada who I seldom saw and I hardly knew my mother who had died when I was only five years old. So, it had always been just the two of us.

Don't get me wrong, I'm not playing the martyr here, my father needed caring for and it was up to me. A nursing home was mentioned but it would have meant selling the house and my father wouldn't hear of it. So, we muddled along as best we could. I had a part-time job at a florist and a nurse popped in once a week. It soon became routine as is usual for many people in that situation.

    Then it happened, very suddenly. I came home from work at about 6.00 clock and I knew as soon as I opened the door that something was wrong; no smell of cooking or the clatter of crockery being laid. It was strangely still and quiet.
    As I opened the door to the lounge I could see my father in his favourite chair, his zimmer upturned and a broken tea cup on the carpet. He was very cold and his lips were slightly blue. I rang the Doctor.

    Well, after the funeral (a quiet affair, just me, the nurse and a neighbor) I had a lot to think about. My father had very little savings and my job didn't pay much so I thought of selling the house. It was far too big for me but it was the only home I'd known, it would be a wrench.
    Then a friend suggested I take in a lodger, perhaps a student or a proffesional person. I wasn't too keen at first but the more I thought about it, I realised it did make sense. The money would be useful of course and it would be company. So I boned up on the internet to learn all I could about rules and regulations etc. I wrote a card out and put it in the local newsagent's window:

Room to let, private shower, shared kitchen, would suit student/professional person.
Please apply box No. 24 for further details.

    Then I thought I had better get the room ready for viewing, my fathers would be ideal. It overlooked the garden and had the sun most of the day.
    A new mattress, fresh linen and new towels were all required. I emptied the wardrobe and chest of drawers (his clothes could all go to the local charity shops). Some new curtains, two nice bright rugs on the polished floor, a large mirror on the far wall and it would be perfect. A small bedside table would be handy and I remembered one I had seen in the

attic. I would go up and have a good look round, I might see some other things that could be used.

I was a little nervous, attics are always spooky places but I was comforted to realise I hadn't heard any strange noises lately.

The door opened with a fearful creak and I stepped inside, right into a nightmare….

A glowing light seemed to hover about a foot in the air and dust motes swirled around. I ran to open the window to get some air and as I turned I could make out some footprints in the dust. They were quite small but clear, shaped like miniature horseshoes and they went towards a cupboard in the corner.

Summing up as much courage as I could, I went towards the corner. The footprints halted about 6 inches from the door. I grasped the handle and screamed in pain and jumped back, my hand burning, instantly turning red and with large painful blisters developing. A strange smell hung in the air and I could hear soft shuffling noises coming from the cupboard. I ran!

Two minutes later I sat trembling at the kitchen table soaking my hand in a bowl of cold water, waiting for the kettle to boil, a mug of hot, sweet tea might calm me.

What had just happened? I asked myself. What was in that attic? In that cupboard? Dare I ever go there again? I'm afraid the answer was a resounding *NO*. I would have to cancel the card in the shop.

Next morning – after a sleepless night – I went to the newsagents and asked him to take the card out.

'Let it, already, have you, that was quick?' asked Ali, smiling.

'Afraid not, I've decided to sell the house instead.' As an afterthought I asked him, 'Ali, do you believe in ghosts?'

'Well, I've always thought that house was a bit spooky, when I used to deliver papers in the early morning there always seemed to be a lot of activity in the attic, faces at the window, children squabbling, you know.'

'But there was only me and Dad,' I said. 'The attic was empty.'

'Well then, you've got your answer,' he said with a nervous smile.

I went to bed that night with plenty to think about and when, at about 3.am, I heard the pitter-patter of tiny feet above me, I switched the lights on and buried my head under the covers until dawn. It was the last night I would spend in that house.

So, there it was, I sold the house very cheaply but I didn't care, it was enough to rent a small flat over the florists shop and I settled in easily.

About a month later I went for a walk after work, it was a pleasant Spring evening. As I rounded a corner two fire engines raced past me, sirens howling. I could see smoke in the distance. My heart sank. As I turned the corner I could see the house was well alight, flames licking at the roof. The attic window was black with soot and I could see four bright eyes, like coals, staring down at me. I blinked and they disappeared as the roof fell in.

I asked a fireman if he knew the cause of the fire and if anyone was hurt.

'It appears to have started in the attic,' he said. 'The owner was out at the time, it's lucky no one was injured. There was one strange thing though,' he hesitated for a moment,'one of my men said as he attempted to get up to the attic, he could hear footsteps running around and terrified sobbing. Yet when he finally got there, there were no signs of anyone. Put the wind up him I think.'

I returned home deep in thought.

I slept badly that night, tossing and turning and I awoke with a throbbing headache. As I put my feet out of bed searching for my slippers I could see tiny horseshoe shaped footprints in the dust. They led to my wardrobe. I could hear the faint pitter-patter of tiny feet and faint laughter coming from the corner.

It would seem they had come looking for a new home………

A Day Out

It was a picture-perfect day, Anna could not have wished for better. She had arrived early to avoid the crowds, it was always so busy on re-enactment days and she didn't like too many people around her.

The moat sparkled as she watched the beautiful swans gliding gracefully by, the rushes bending slowly in the soft summer breeze, the wonderful scent drifting over from the rose garden.

Her own ornate be-jewelled outfit was a little too heavy for a sunny day like today but it was too late to change into something lighter.

She decided to head to the Maze, it always brought back many happy memories of her childhood, when she would come with her mother who would tease her by calling out her name as the sound always echoed strangely and appeared to come from all directions at once, she would scream with delight at such fun.

She saw some more people in the distance, probably watching the falconry display, but they were far away and would not disturb her. It wasn't that she was anti social but she did prefer her own company most of the time. It meant she could reminisce to her hearts content, even talk to herself if she wanted to (as she often did).

She entered the maze and was immediately overwhelmed by the size of it, no matter how many times she had been there. The hedges were very high and she was quite short, so it always seemed rather dark and forbidding.

Anna rounded a corner and to her dismay, saw a party of school children heading her way, but she could not avoid them. They seemed to shimmer in the morning light, almost transparent and their voices echoed slightly. They giggled as they squeezed past, all dressed in Tudor outfits.

'Good morrow, m'lady,' said their teacher, bowing slightly as they drew level, 'Tis a fine morning, is it not?'

'Y,Yes' stammered Anna, blushing slightly, 'Why did they talk like that?' she wondered. 'I suppose they are role playing, all part of the fun, living history I think they call it.'

After leaving the Maze, she headed towards the formal gardens all laid out in intricate geometric patterns. She chose a seat to rest on and enjoy the view of the castle itself, it really was quite splendid, no wonder so many people liked to visit on such a fine day.

A portly middle-aged man, dressed in a splendid regalia with a beautiful velvet cap trimmed with peacock feathers sat down beside her. He smiled warmly. He looked very familiar but then most of the people here today tended to look the same, many were dressed in a similar fashion..

From the open windows of the castle she could hear the gentle sound of lutes and virginals, she closed her eyes fo ra moment and nodded off. She awoke with a start and shivered slightly. Although the sun was still quite bright, a chill breeze had sprung up. It might be warmer inside, she thought.

Entering through a very heavy, ornately carved door, Anna came to the splendour of the Great Hall. There were dancers in elaborate costumes and masques who seemed to float most gracefully across the floor. There were many intricate steps, bows and little hops. Much laughter and flirting abounded.

Her eye was caught by a splendid table at the far end of the room, slightly raised. It was groaning with food of every description; pheasants, a huge turkey, hams, sweet breads, spiced apples and oranges, flagons of ales and a huge pie with blackbirds poking out of the crust. It made her mouth water.

All the ladies sparkled with heavily jewelled head dresses and magnificent gowns but it was the man in the centre who caught her eye and she stared in amazement, it was the same man who had sat beside her on the bench, he looked extremely regal.

'This must be a dream', she thought, 'I must be hallucinating.'

Suddenly, the view in front of her seemed to shimmer and she felt quite faint. All the colours seemed to fade to a dull grey and one by one, the people around her disappeared until she was left alone in a large empty room.

Her heart pounded with fear as a sudden truth revealed itself and bitter tears rolled down her cheeks. She turned towards a long, gilded mirror set by the door. A silent scream filled her lungs, there was no reflection! She walked closer and the glass shimmered and enveloped her as she passed quietly through to the invisible world she had come from.

Later, on the bus home, the children who had been in the Maze were chatting.

'Did you see that strange lady that we passed?' said one small girl, 'she looked just like a picture in my history book about the Tudors, she was the one who had her head chopped off.'

'I think you have had a little too much sun, Ophelia,' said her teacher,' there are no such things as ghosts. It was just another re-enactor, but a good one I must admit. Next thing you'll be saying you saw Henry the Eighth as well,' and she chuckled to herself.

'Yes Miss, well as a matter of fact I……….'

'Enough, Ophelia, I said that's quite enough, now let's all settle down, it's been a long day ' said the teacher crossly.

Ophelia said no more, but it would be a long time before she would forget this particular day out.

Gloria Hobson

Salvation

The sun was merciless, Sam had never felt such heat, every breath he took hurt his lungs and he could feel his skin tightening and blistering. He must find some shade soon or he must surely die.
It was like being set alight with a blow torch, how had this come about?

One minute he was riding along the trail on Bella, his faithful old mare, and the next he was coming too on a pile of boulders, his horse nowhere to be seen. His left leg was obviously broken and he had some cuts on his face from when he had been ejected from the saddle.

He looked around. He was only about 20 miles from home but it might as well be 200. His phone had been in his saddle bag along with some water and an old blanket. But his horse had disappeared, probably ran off in fright.

If any one else was around there was the slim chance his horse might be seen and a search party organised. But he knew that was hardly likely. No one would miss him until Monday morning when he failed to turn up in the office. His home was quite isolated, on the edge of the desert, and any family he had lived back east and were seldom in touch. All in all, the outlook seemed pretty bleak.

He heard a screech overhead and a golden eagle looked down at him with pity – thank God it wasn't a vulture, he thought with a grimace. Sam looked around, he wasn't going to give up just yet.

Then he thought he saw a flash in the distance. Perhaps he was hallucinating, dehydration could do that to a person, he had read somewhere. But then he saw it again. What could it be? He asked himself.

Sam wasn't a particularly religious person, he hardly ever went to church, but you know what they say, 'there are no atheists in foxholes', so he hoped to God whatever it was would be his salvation.

As the flashing got closer, he rubbed his eyes and blinked. It was a silver ball, high in the sky, a little like a Christmas bauble glittering high above him and it was heading in his direction.

He tried to sit up, then screamed in agony as pain shot through his damaged leg. Then he felt a drop of water fall onto his face, then another, he gazed upwards and could hardly believe what he was seeing

The silver ball was about 50 feet above him and cool water was falling straight on to his face. He opened his mouth to catch as much as he could, belief was suspended, all he could feel was gratitude, thanks to whatever miracle he was witnessing. 'Thankyou God' he muttered', was he going mad?

But no, the water was real, very real.

Then as suddenly as it had started, it stopped and when he looked up the ball had disappeared, but the welcome drink had re-juvenated him and gave him a little more strength to face his ordeal.

He would try to crawl to a small overhang a short distance away where there would be some shade.

Every inch was agony, it was like pulling himself over shards of glass, but he finally made it and lay gasping and exhausted.

What had just happened? he thought. Was it a dream, had he lost his mind? His eyes closed and sleep overcame him.

He awoke suddenly to feel a large, hairy tongue licking his face. It was Bella, she had come back, thank the Lord. He reached for his water bottle and took a careful sip, he would have to ration it carefully. The horse could get some moisture from the long grass in the shade under the rocks. It would be dark soon and, although it was unbelievably hot during the day, at night it could get extremely cold. He called Bella towards him and he managed to get the old horse blanket off her back and wrapped it tightly around himself. His phone fell out of his saddle bag but it was badly broken so was no use at all.

It got dark very quickly and already he could see lots of stars; it was going to be a long night……

He dozed fitfully, the night seemed to go on forever and when he finally opened his eyes it was to see the most bizarre sight. High in the misty clouds, just a few feet above him, was a giant bird, the enormous wings casting a huge shadow over him. I must have died, he thought with sadness. This must be an angel coming to swoop me up to heaven. A brilliant light hurt his eyes.

If this is death, it isn't too bad, I just wish I could have lived little longer, maybe married and had a family. He lapsed into semi-conciousness and the next sensation was one of floating towards the stars, floating through the clouds, up and up, towards Heaven.

The brilliant light hurt his eyes, his lids too almost too heavy to open. An angel all in white loomed over him and held his hand, then another appeared and pressed something cold against his chest. He struggled weakly and tried to push them away, then everything went black again.

'Mr King, Sam, wake up! Hello Sam, come on, open your eyes.' With a great effort Sam managed to open his eyes to see two pretty nurses, both in white uniforms. He blinked.

'Where am I? Am I in Heaven?'

One of the nurses smiled. 'You're in St. Aidens Emergency room, Sam. You've had a bit of a shock, do you remember anything?'

'I fell off my horse and then I died,' Sam muttered, 'I don't understand what's happening'.

'Well, you didn't die Sam, but you were very lucky. A routine helicopter patrol spotted your horse running free and they followed her to where you were sheltering. They dropped some large water balloons to you and returned the next morning when it was light enough to winch you up and here you are, quite simple, no miracles or anything supernatural. Your horse was collected later and is being looked after by a local farmer.'

So there it was. Sam stayed in hospital for a couple of weeks until his leg was strong enough for him to be allowed home. All in all he did feel very lucky and, despite what the nurses had told him he still felt there had been some sort of divine intervention and he was sure God had heard him and came to his rescue, (and Bella, of course).

Gloria Hobson

All Hallowes

From the Isle of Wight to the Isle of Skye
'Trick or Treat' is the oft heard cry,
Across the world kids will holler
Just to get an extra dollar.

But beyond the jest and playful fun
Ghosts await the setting sun
When long dead spirits, free for a night
Give honest folk a dreadful fright.

Chains will rattle, bones will jangle
Skulls will grin and cobwebs dangle.
Best lock your door, take to your bed
And pull tight the covers O'er your head.

Trick or Treat

Being a gravedigger was no laughing matter at the best of times let alone as Halloween approached, thought Bert as he stood in the churchyard contemplating the hard ground in front of him. It was a bit of a last minute rush, the funeral had been brought forward to 11.30 the next day and it was already 2.00 clock, it would be getting dark in a couple of hours.

He had better get a move on, he especially wanted to be done before the local schools finished and all the kids came sauntering down the lane on their way home into the village.

All week they had been teasing him as he tidied up the verges and swept the leaves into neat piles prior to burning. A masked face would suddenly pop up over the wall, startling him or a plastic skeleton would be hanging from a tree branch.

Although he should be used to it by now, it still unnerved him and he was always glad to get home to his tiny cottage behind the church where he could enjoy a nice cup of tea and a bacon sandwich.

A country churchyard with tumbledown gravestones was bound to be a magnet for the local miscreants but one boy in particular seemed to relish frightening people. His name was Wayne, he was 13 and he already had a reputation as a trouble-maker.

As usual he was playing truant so he decided he would pay Bert a visit and put the fear of God up the old geezer. He had a new mask he had pinched from the market – like Dracula, with long white fangs. That should do the trick and he set off towards the church, grinning mischeviously.

    The grave was coming along nicely, once the turf was off the underlying earth wasn't too bad, Bert was already four foot down and he straightened up as his aging back started to twinge painfully.
    Suddenly, a low growl came from behind him and, as he turned, a creature with a white face and sharp fangs launched itself at him, sinking his teeth into Bert's scrawny neck. They went tumbling into the grave together, blood spurting everywhere, Bert passing out instantly whilst the fiend drank his fill.

    Wayne climbed silently over the wall and made his way towards the pile of soil wondering where Bert could be, probably gone for a tea break he thought. He crept towards the hole and peered over the edge. The creature looked up in surprise, blood running down his chin.
    'Gosh Trev, you gave me a fright,' said Wayne, 'where did you gey that mask from? I thought you were at school today. Surprised the old beggar, did you?' and he chortled to himself.
    Trev stood up and Wayne stepped forward to help his friend out only to stare at the sharp claws that dug into his hands.
    'Ouch!' he exclaimed, 'got some fancy gloves as well, did you?' and he looked more closely at him, his eyes widening in sudden terror as the realisation dawned that the thing in front of him was not Trev.
    The vide-like grip tightened as Wayne tried to pull away and his last sight before he passed screaming into the next world, was of sharp fangs bearing down on him.

    At 4.00 the noisy parade of children came down the lane, all chattering excitedly about the 'trick or treating' to be enjoyed later. As they passed the churchyard, some older boys noticed the partly dug grave and went to investigate.

'Hey, come over here.' They shouted excitedly to the others, 'There are two full-size monster dummies down here, we can hawk them around with us tonight, that'll scare everyone, come and help us to pull them out'.

From behind a nearby yew tree, a dark figure with glowing eyes watched, waited and licked his lips in anticipation.

Gloria Hobson

The Scales of Justice

The Scales of Justice can swing both ways depending on which side you happen to be on. Let me tell you about a case I was involved in some time ago and you will see what I mean.

After Uni - where I studied Law - I was lucky enough to get a position as a Junior Clerk at a Law Firm which specialised in criminal matters. It was quite a large practice and the work was varied.

One day, the Senior Partner asked me if I would like to do some work on a new case that had just come in. The background was that a young man from a very respectable family, had driven into a petrol station, filled up his car and drove off without paying. It seemed fairly clear cut as it was all caught on CCTV, his number plate was quite visible, so it was easy for the Police to track him down.

But, there was one problem, he had a watertight alibi!

His name was Jacob Goldberg, a medical student, and he said he had been at home all night with his girlfriend, Leah. This wasn't something he would normally do as his parents were quite strict. But they had gone away for the weekend to a small cottage they owned in the Lake District. His girlfriend could verify this, of course.

An appointment was arranged for them to come into the Office later that day and I was to do the initial interview. His parents would also be there, an affluent couple, both doctors at a local private hospital, their son wanted to follow in their footsteps and a criminal record would ruin that, of course.

At 10.30 sharp, Mr and Mrs Goldberg, Jacob and Leah arrived and were shown into an interview room. They all seemed very confident that this matter would be sorted out quickly.

After the initial pleasantries, we got down to business. I explained about the CCTV footage and asked their views but Jacob, who seemed to me to be a little arrogant, insised it must be a case of mistaken identity.

' Perhaps the car was stolen and later replaced in the driveway,' suggested Mr Goldberg. Highly unlikely of course, why steal a car and bring it back?

According to the Police, the only fingerprints in the car were Jacobs. I had seen the film earlier and, although it was a little grainy, the number plate was quite clear and the driver had a strong resemblance to Jacob.

Yet, it made me uneasy, they seemed a genuine, respectable family, not the type to lie outright especially to a Solicitor. I took as much information as I could and we parted company an hour later. I told them I would speak to my Seniors and get back to them as soon as possible.

Something was not quite right about all this but I could not see any way round it, the evidence was quite clear and the Police were keen to get the matter to Court. It was hard to reconcile the CCTV evidence with the couple's insistence that they were both at home, there was no one to back that up.

Then I thought about CCTV at the house (assuming they had it). It was a large detached house in an affluent area so it would be a magnet for the local criminal fraternity. I rang Mr Goldberg and he did indeed say they had CCTV and he would bring it in so we could all view it. They arrived within the hour and we all sat down to view it together, feeling a little optimistic that this might clear the matter up, once and for all.

Unfortnately not, the footage showed a young man coming round the side of the house, getting into a car and driving it away. It was not possible to be certain who it was.

Then Jacob had a sudden brainwave. He had completely forgotten that he and Leah had ordered a take-away from the local tandoori outlet. He couldn't remember the exact time but that should be quite easy to check up on, they always kept records of all those sort of transactions.

A quick phone call verified a meal had been delivered that night, the exact time was 10.15 and it had been caught on the drivers cell phone camera which they always used for security reasons.

Looking at the Police notes, the car had been at the garage at 10.10pm so it would have been impossible for Jacob to have been in two places at once, or was it?

I didn't know what to think, it was a real puzzle, both films were genuine but contained conflicting information.

Of course, we contacted the Police and they were just as puzzled. Because of the discrepancy in the evidence, it was decided to drop the charges unless anything else came to light. The Defendent had to get the benefit of the doubt, so the matter was reluctantly put to bed and filed away. It would have to remain a mystery.

But then 6 months later, the police were called to the Goldberg house after a call from Jacob. Both Mr and Mrs Goldberg were found dead in the basement in what looked like a murder/suicide.

Of course, it came as a shock to us all, how much could one family take?

According to Jacob, he had come home from college and assumed his parents must be out visiting friends, Leah had arrived for tea as she did every Wednesday. They both settled down to do some homework at the kitchen table.

The house was quite cold so Jacob decided to put the central heating on- the main switch was in the basement. Then he made the horrific dscovery of his parents bodies, a shot gun lay nearby, it was a very unpleasant sight.

The Police attended, the Coroner was informed and an inquest would be held in due course. All the facts pointed to a murder/suicide though no one could think of a reason. It is true, of course, that no one can really know what goes on behind closed doors.

We, the Firm that is, sent a letter of condolence and Jacob rang to thank us and said we were welcome to attend the funeral if we wished to, I said I would go.

The service was held in the local Synagogue and was well attended, they were a well respected couple in the community and would be missed greatly. Afterwards, we all went back to the house for refreshments and Leah came over to me.

' Jacob says thankyou for coming,' he's too upset to talk to anyone at the moment.'

'Of course,' I said sympathetically, 'he's had a lot to put up with lately, hasn't he?'

Leah hesitated. 'Yes, I suppose so, but their's more to this than meets the eye.'

'What do you mean?' I asked.

She looked over her shoulder nervously, Jacob was talking animatedly to the Rabbi and hadn't noticed her with me. Is there something bothering you?' I asked quietly.

Tear sprang to her eyes and she blinked them away furiously.

'I can't talk now, could you meet me later, do you? If I don't talk to someone soon I think I will go mad.'

So, we arranged to meet for lunch the next day. I didn't tell anyone in the Office initially, I would see what she had to say first.

The next day at 12.30 I sat waiting in a small restaurant, wondering if she would appear. At 12.40 she arrived, looking very pretty in a pale grey suit, we ordered a light meal and I sat patiently to listen to what she had to say.

The night of the petrol theft debacle was simple. Apparently his parents were very strict with money, he was only given a small allowance and when he asked for more it just created awful arguments. They said it was character building, he said they were just mean.

Well, he needed some petrol, the tank was almost empty. So, he hatched a plan. To give himself an alibi he arranged for a take-away to be delivered at 10.15. Leah would stay at home to take delivery while he was at the garage filling up his car. When she answered the door she called out behind her, 'The takeaway's here, I'll get it,' to obviously give the impression he was in the house with her.

It was a simple plan that worked quite well, although Leah wasn't too happy about her part in it.

But, the question of money still caused tension with his parents and the situation worsened, many angry confrontations ensued. There was only one way to settle it, at least to his way of thinking.

Meanwhile Leah became more and more nervous as his behaviour seemed to change drastically. He ranted on about them all the time, about all the money they had and he often said he wished they were dead. This upset Leah, of course, as his mother and father had been nothing but kind and courteous to her. She became more and more worried about Jacob.

She paused to take a sip of water and to pick at her salad. I sat entranced by it all, realising that this conversation should not be taking place at all. But I didn't want it to stop, I think it took an awful lot of courage to tell me all this and I admired her for it.

She continued: 'The night of the killing, I called as usual, just after tea and he told me his parents must be out with friends as they were not at home when he arrived from college. I thought no more about it, but then, when he made the 'discovery' in the basement, all sorts of warning bells went off.

For a start, instead of hysterical tears which I would have expected he seemed strangely cold and distant.'

Then she knew what she had to do, she must find someone to confide in and that someone was me. It wasn't absolute proof, of course and if he was confronted he would most likely make up a tissue of lies to cover himself.

The first thing we must do, I told her, was inform the Police, so we left the restaurant immediately. On the way we called at my Office and brought them up to date, they agreed we should report it all to the Police and then I should let them know the outcome.

Well, the ending was a bit of an anti climax.
Jacob was arrested the follwing day on suspicion of murder which he strongly denied, of course.
However Leah's statement shook him considerably, he thought his girlfriend would never betray him, but she was a decent girl and her conscience got the better of her.
At the Trial, some months later, he refused to take the stand and pleaded Not Guilty. However, the many arguments about money plus the lies about the petrol theft and Leah's statement about him wishing his parents dead, his anger towards them all conspired against him. He changed his plea to Guilty and he was given the mandatory life sentence with the Judge's recommendation he serve at least 30 years

So, all the silly talk about doubles was nonsense, there was nothing paranormal about this case. It was a straightforward case of greed overcoming anything.
I beathed a sigh of relief and to a certain extent, sadness. Partly for the horrifying death of two good people and also for the waste of his own life. He could have made a success of it had not his temper got the better of him.
As for Leah, we remained friends and still see each other occasionally. I wish her every happiness for the future.

Gloria Hobson

Let Sleeping Dogs Lie

Many years ago when I was a 17 year old schoolgirl, our French teacher, Madame Dupont, suggested that myself and 5 other girls who were going to take 'A level French later that year, would benefit from an exchange scheme we had with our French counterparts.

We set off in high spirits on the ferry from Dover to Calais, then on to our final destination in north east France, a small village near Sedan on the river Meuse.

We were to stay at a farm and three days a week we would attend the local Lycee, it was all very pleasant and it was made even more pleasant because the farmer had two sons, Alain who was 18 and Pierre who was 19. All the girls had a crush on them though their mother Madame Marchand, kept a strict eye on all of us.

We soon settled into a routine. We girls shared a large attic bedroom, meals were typically French – fresh rolls every day, lots of cheese and fruit, we were allowed one glass of wine with our evening meal. This we found so exciting, we would never have been allowed this at home, so we felt very sophisticated.

The Lycee was pretty similar to our own Grammar School, fairly strict and we could speak nothing but French, even between ourselves. After all, that was what we came for. Back at the farm the two boys liked to speak English as they were just as keen to pass their own exams. We all got along quite well. Monsieur Marchand kept himself to himself, he was a man of few words who was busy on the farm most of the time.

One weekend we were asked if we would like to go with the boys for a picnic in the nearby Argonne forest, a local beauty spot so we borrowed some push bikes and set off with our packed lunches
I had an old-fashioned box Brownie camera (this was the fifties after all), that my father had given to me. I wanted to take as many mementos as possible of this once-in-a-lifetme experience.
A peaceful spot near the river looked ideal and we spread our blankets on the grass and went for a paddle, the two boys splashing us playfully. I caught sight of a ruined house nearby and wandered over to take a closer look and I took a few photos and then moved round to the side where I was startled to see a young man resting on a wall. He didn't see me at first so I snapped a quick photo of him.
'Bonjour,' I said, trying out my schoolgirl French, 'comment allez vous?'
He smiled, 'I can tell you are English by your accent,' he said.
Slightly embarrassed, I sat down on a nearby tree trunk
'Are you staying nearby?' he asked politely.
'Yes, at a farm, we are on a school exchange trip to try to improve our French, come and join us if you like, we are over there by the river,' and I pointed over my shoulder.
'Thankyou, but I must go, my comrades will be waiting for me,' and he got up to leave and disappeared round the corner of the building.
I went back to my friends and we ate our lunch. 'Where did you get to?' asked Alain.
I told him about the young man I had seen near the ruins. He seemed puzzled but said nothing.

The afternoon passed very pleasantly but then we could see some dark clouds in the distance and hear the faint rumbling of thunder, so we decided to head for home and just made it before the heavens opened.
Madam Marchand asked if we had had a good day and we all agreed it had been 'tres bien'. I said I had taken lots of photos and when I got them developed I would show them to her. She pointed behind her to a very old,

very heavy, highly polished dresser that every French home seemed to possess.

'We have a lot of photographs here of our family, some are of the boys when they were young.' She took one down to show me, the boys looked really cute, I would say they were about two years old.

Another one caught my eye. 'And who is this?' I asked. She hesitated and looked quite sad for a moment.

'That was my brother, Alphonse, he died during La Guerre in 1916, there was a lot of fighting around here you know. His whole unit was blown up by a landmine, there wasn't even a proper funeral. So we just have our memories.' She passed it to me.

I looked closely at the photograph and almost dropped it with shock. Alphonse was the young man I had seen near the ruined house by the river. I must have gone very pale because Madam put her arm around me.

'Are you ill, ma cherie?' she asked, looking very concerned.

'N,No,' I stuttered, 'I'm just a bit tired, it has been a long day.'

'Then you should all go to bed,' she insisted and she ushered us up the stairs to the attic.

The next day Alain gestured to me to join him in the garden after breakfast.

'Did you recognise Uncle Alphonse in that photograph?' he asked quietly.

'Yes,' I replied, there seemed no point in denying it.

'Let me tell you, you aren't the only one to have seen him in that particular spot, I've seen him twice but have never actually spoken to him. Of course, I didn't tell Mother as it would only upset her too much. They were very close as children, I don't think she ever got over the shock of it at all, though it is a long time ago now, best let sleeping dogs lie. I doubt she would believe me anyway. All the same I am glad you saw him because at least it proves it was not my imagination.'

So there it was. Our time eventually came to an end and we returned home to England with many happy memories. I told no one about the photo, I had them all developed and sent some to Alain to remind him of our time there and asked him to thank his mother for her hospitality.

I kept the one of Alphonse in a drawer in my night dresser and sometimes I get it out to look at and try to imagine the young man from all those years ago.

'Bon nuit, Alphonse,' I whisper, 'dormir bien.'

Gloria Hobson

The Waiting Room

Jack shivered as he walked carefully along the canal side. The path was covered in leaves and was very slippery. He really could not remember how he got here but that was not unusual, at 82 he often had memory lapses. He would head for home, try to get dry and have a nice warm drink before going to bed.

He looked up, the clouds were drifting away and some bright stars could be seen. He came to an old iron gate that would lead into the town. He could see, across the road, a small building with bright lights shining through the windows.

I'll head for there, he thought, *maybe I can rest for a while and try to unscramble my mind. It may be a pub or a cafe, I can ask for some directions.* He really did not know this part of town very well.

He could hear voices murmuring quietly as he pushed the door open. It was warm and cosy, there were about a dozen people sat around so he found himself a seat in a corner, next to a young girl who seemed to have a nasty cut on her head. She turned away obviously not wanting to make small talk.

Suddenly a door opened, a voice called out a name and an elderly lady with a walking stick hobbled across and disappeared down a long corridor.

He looked around, all the people seemed to appear to be quite poorly. This must be one of those emergency drop-in clinics for those needing attention for minor injuries, out of hours they called it.

'Well,' he thought, 'there's really nothing wrong with me, I'm just a bit wet, as soon as I'm dry, I'll get on home.'

But it was quite cosy and very soon he began to feel sleepy and before long, he nodded off.

Suddenly, he felt someone nudging him and he awoke with a start. A middle aged man in a smart suit, clutching a brief case, smiled at him. 'Have you been waiting long?' he asked.

'I don't really know,' Jack replied, looking around; most of the people seemed to have gone.

'It's a strange place, don't you think?' the man said, 'Not at all what I expected.'

'What do you mean?' Jack asked, puzzled.

'Well, when they talk about God's waiting room, I didn't really expect it to look like a proper waiting room.'

'I'm not sure what you mean,' replied Jack, a sudden fear gripping him.

The stranger gave him a look full of sadness and compassion. 'You really don't know? Well, I'm sorry to be the one to tell you, but we are all dead, I myself suffered a catastrophic heart attack at the office, overwork and overweight, I suppose.'

Jack's eyes widened with horror, 'But I don't feel dead,' he stuttered.

'Well, you look very wet to me, it's a fine night, do you think you might have fallen in the canal and drowned?'

Jack had a sudden flash of memory. Something about tripping over a tree root, then being enveloped in dark, muddy water and getting himself tangled up in a rusty old supermarket trolley. There was no pain, just a sadness that it should all end this way. His eyes filled with tears.

Suddenly the far door opened and a voice called out, 'Next please.'

There were only the two of them left.

'Shall we go through together?' asked the gentleman at his side, 'it may not seem as frightening then.'

So, Jack stood up, they took a deep breath and walked with dignity through the door. All fear left them both as they followed the light and disappeared quietly into Eternity.

Gloria Hobson

The Rocker

As soon as she saw the rocking chair in the dealers window, Rhoda Mason knew she had to have it. It was just perfect, exactly what she had been looking for since she moved into her small cottage in the Welsh countryside. Despite its apparent age, it looked very sturdy, made from highly polished hardwood with a beautifully carved back with such fine detail it almost looked like lace.

Impatiently she went inside to ask the price. To her surprise it was a lot less than she had expected, the man explained he wanted to make space for new stock and seemed almost relieved to get rid of it.
He would deliver it the next day.

Hurrying home she immediately moved things around to accomodate her new aquisition, she wanted it near to the fire and in front of the window. She moved a small table next to it and, to complete the look, picked some fresh flowers from the tiny garden to set on it. Perfect.

Promptly at ten the next morning the chair was delivered and put in place. A large flowered cushion made it look very homely and she sank down on to it with a contented sigh. Rocking gently she called for her large tabby cat – Cleo- to sit on her lap but one look at the rocker and she hissed loudly and ran away. Never mind, she would soon get used to it.

After 10 mintes Rhoda suddenly felt very nauseous and light headed and she went into the kitchen for a glass of water. She remembered that she hadn't had any breakfast that morning, a slice of toast would put things right. She soon felt better and, as it was quite a pleasant day, she went out into the garden to prepare the small vegetable patch she was hoping to cultivate.

It had been a big step for her to move from the large industrial town in the North to this small village deep in the forested heart of mid-Wales. But early retirement from the bank and a decent pension meant she could finally realise her dream of a cottage in the country. She loved the quietness, solitude and beautiful views from her window and she was truly content.

After tea she went back into the small sitting room, picked up a newspaper and settled into her new rocker, the fire was glowing faintly and the sun was starting to set. She put her head back and dozed lightly, wondering vaguely where Cleo could be.

Suddenly Rhoda sat bolt upright as what felt like an electric shock passed through her, almost falling off the chair. She jumped up and looked around her, it was almost dark and as she looked out of the window, she was startled to see two large yellow eyes staring at her.

'Cleo!' she called and opened the window. The cat jumped through, carefully avoiding the chair.

'Come on, let's have an early night, I don't feel very well,' and she went upstairs and, undressing quickly, crawled into bed with Cleo across her feet.

She slept fitfully, the night interspersed with strange dreams and she awoke with a thumping headache and double vision. Downstairs Rhoda thought back to when she had first felt unwell and she glanced suspiciously at the chair, what could it be? Perhaps it had been treated with some chemicals to prevent woodworm or maybe a strong varnish had been used. Yes, that must be it. She walked across the room to examine it but she couldn't smell anything strange, just the faint aroma of beeswax polish.

Rhoda peered at the intricate carvings on the back, they seemed full of strange symbols and curliques and with sudden inspiration she reached for a note pad and copied them as best she could. After breakfast she would catch a bus to the nearest town wher she knew there was a good antiquarian bookshop on the High Street, perhaps she could find a book which might explain their meaning.

By 10.30 she was in the shop searching among the dusty shelves, there were quite a few books on Masonic symbols and Egyptian hieroglyphics, not quite what she was looking for. She was about to give up when, tucked away at the rear, was a book called 'Ancient Rituals and Symbols of Satanic Origins'.

She flicked through the pages and turned to a chapter called Signs of the Beast and her heart almost stopped. There, in front of her, was a symbol that looked very familiar. Digging out the piece of paper from her pocket, she held it against the page. Realising that she had drawn it upside down she turned it around to see that it was exactly the same. What she had taken for elaborate carvings were, in fact, numbers – 666. She knew their significance, of course, she remembered them from her Sunday School days, something to do with the Devil. She shuddered and felt quite cold even though it was very stuffy in the shop. Paying the owner she hurried out for the bus home.

Rhoda sat at the kitchen table with a steaming cup of hot chocolate with the book in front of her, willing herself to open it. Though it was only 3.00 o'clock, it was already getting dark and a light rain pattered against the window. She turned to the page with the illusrations and read the text at the side:

666 is considered by some to be the mark of the Beast or the Devil (see Revelations, chapter 13, verse18) and is sometmes used to invoke his presence. To treat it lightly can have dangerous consequences. The Beast will wreak vengeance on all who mock his name name.

She had read enough, the chair would have to go. A sudden flash of lightening lit up the darkening skies and thunder rumbled across the nearby hills. The light flickered and went out and the house suddenly became very gloomy. Searching under the sink Rhoda found a torch and some candles, not much but it would have to do. Puling her cardigan around her thin shoulders she opened the back door and called for Cleo, there was no sign of her, she was probably sheltering in the garden shed.

A noise from the living room caught her attention and she strode nervously across and opened the door quietly, torch in hand. The chair was rocking gently in what seemed ike a misty haze, she shook her head and tried to move back but her feet were frozen to the ground, then the torch tumbled from her hand plunging the room into semi-darkness. A low moan escaped from her lips as her terror increased and a vague outline seemed to shimmer on the chair.

A figure sat there but it was too indistinct to tell who or what it was. The rocking became faster and faster, creaking loudly on the polished wood floor and Rhoda thought she would surely lose her mind.
Then the rocking stopped and a loud clap of thunder almost deafened her, the dark form rose from the chair and turned to face her, a putrid stench overwhelming her nostrils.

The face was like nothing she could have ever imagined in her worst nightmares, dark features but with eyes that glowed like red hot coals, a scarlet slash for a mouth with a black tongue lolling out, green spittle drooling down the chin. He moved towards her seeming almost to float and he held out his arms to embrace her, his long curled talons digginginto her back as he held her close. The room began to swim and her senses finally left her as she sank unconcious onto the floor.

Something was licking her face and her eyes flickered open. It was Cleo leaning over her purring loudly, her fishy breath making her retch. She sat up shivering and glanced around her. It was daylight, she must have lain there all night. She looked across to the corner, the rocker sat there seeming perfectly innocent. What had happened last night? Was it a dream? Rhoda wasn't sure. Had she passed out?

She struggled to her feet and approached the chair. As she leaned over to touch it a faint tingle ran up her arm and when she looked down she could see two deep grooves on the floor as though someone heavy had been rocking violently. Her blood ran cold. She knew what must be done.

She approached the rocker, it looked completely harmless as she dragged it outside, hesitating for a moment but then she remembered last night and was convinced she was doing the right thing.

Within half an hour the pieces were piled up on the empty vegetable patch, some paraffin was sprinkled over and a lit match sent flames high into the air. Rhoda watched for some minutes until the heat drove her back inside and a strange smell of sulphur filled the air.

Closing the door she bent to stroke Cleo. 'Come on, old girl, let's get you something to eat,' she said, and they went inside.

Behind her, in the depths of the fire, a low cackle could be heard and two deep red coals burned menacingly in her direction.

Kismet

All good things must come to an end, so they say, but does that apply to all bad things as well?

I sincerely hope so for, if not, the men in white coats will be taking me away soon. Let me tell you why.

A year ago, my parents were both killed in a dreadful car accident whilst on holiday in Germany.

Travelling down the autobahn to Heidleberg - a fine university town - they called into a service station for fuel and, whilst re-joining the main road, foolishly drove onto the wrong side and were killed instantly. I found this hard to believe because they had driven on the Continent for years. But it only takes a moments inattention for tragedy to strike.

The only reason I tell you this is because this seemed to be the starting point for just one bad thing after another. I am not normally superstitious but I definitely think something strange is going on.

My girlfriend, Anita, who I had known for about 5 years, suddenly left me for my best friend and about a month later she had a big win on the Lottery! Good luck for her of course, but not for me.

Then the advertising firm I worked for sold out to a major competitor and I was let go as I was 'surplus to requirements'. A week later, cycling to the Job Centre to sign on, I was knocked off my bike by a white van man who failed to stop. I broke my left ankle and was in plaster for a month.

I thought I might be able to make a living from home with a bit of freelance work but the country was in the middle of a slump, so it all came to nothing

My brother Sam, called me a moaning minnie and told me to stop feeling sorry for myself. Why not try something completely different. He was right, of course.

Then, one day while perusing the local rag, I spotted an advertisement in the jobs section. It read:

Wanted, steady, reliable man/woman for varied work in the entertainment field. Please apply Box No. 13

What could 'entertainment field' mean? I wondered. It coverered quite a wide spectrum. But, nothing ventured, nothing gained as they say. So I sent a letter and CV and sat back to wait.

It didn't take long for a reply to come back and I was invited in for an interview the next day.

The address was on a shabby looking side street, between a massage parlour and a bookies. The office was at the top of a rickety staircase, a faint aroma of cat pee permeated the air. A man was waiting for me. He was dressed all in black and he was very gaunt, cadaverous you might say.

But his handshake was firm and his smile was genuine. He introduced himself as Karol, he had a very slight east European accent. I sat down on a black, plastic chair and listened to what he had to say.

An hour later I left feeling quite re-juvenated, he said I was just what he was looking for to join him on a new venture. Could I start a week later? Of course I said yes.

As for a job description, now that is a difficult one. Suffice it to say the work would be varied, the hours irregular (mostly at night). I would have to be broad minded, open to new ideas and experiences.

He said he liked my enthusiasm. I hoped it would last.

The starting date arrived, I was to meet him outside his office at 9.30pm. Being October, it was already dark and there weren't many people about. He had a small black van and I hopped in.

We drove out of town, after about 10 miles we pulled off the main road down a dark country lane and pulled up around the back of a large house. We parked quietly and surveyed the scene. There were a few lights on but mainly at the front and they were very dim.

Our equipment was all in the back, we dressed quickly and quietly. He had a notebook in his hand which he kept referring to and he ran through once again, the part I had to play in the proceedings that would follow shortly.

We entered silently through the unlocked back door, I could hear faint voices coming from the front room. Moving stealthily we carried our gear inside. The door to the main room had been left slightly ajar and it was covered on the inside by a heavy black curtain.

At a signal from Karol I set a small fan going silently behind the curtain which moved very slightly. Then I increased the movement so the curtains stirred a little more and suddenly there was silence from the other room. At another signal from Karol, I switched the electricity off and everywhere was plunged into total darkness.

A scream came from someone which was hushed by a man's voice.

The next piece of equipment was a small tape recorder and I was told to switch it on quietly,

A dog's bark could be heard and a man's voice called out; 'Be quiet, Aldo!' it echoed slightly.

Now, heart-wrenching sobs came from the front room and I was instructed to move a switch up and down so that all the lights flickered. The next item on the tape was a loud clap of thunder which even made me jump. Silence reigned for a moment and then quiet voices could be heard, soothing voices to quell the hysterical tears.

And that was the end of the performance, we moved our equipment quietly out to the van. The last duty for me was to go back in and turn on all the lights. We drove home quietly, I was still feeling a bit nervous when Karol asked me, 'How do you feel after our first engagement?'

I hardly knew what to say. 'Are they all going to be like this?' I muttered.

'It varies according to the individual requirements, of course. The medium will give me some details of the deceased and I tailor it to fit around that. Most of it is pretty general but I always try to put in little touches to give it authenticity, like the dog there, the husband was killed taking the dog for a walk. They were both run over by a stolen car. It's little details like that that does the trick. You'd be surprised how many people believe in that sort of thing.'

'I suppose they must get some comfort from it,' I said thoughtfully. But I didn't like to think they were being conned. I soon got over that, though, when my first pay cheque arrived. My early scruples soon disappeared and Karol was a very generous employer. My official title was Assistant Grief Counsellor – Stretching the truth a bit, I know.

Well time passed, all the routines were fairly similar and the work was more regular than I thought it would be. Then after 6 months, I turned as usual but Karol was nowhere to be seen. I tried the office door but it was locked. He never told me where he lived or gave me his private phone number so there was not a lot I could do.

After a few days, a headline in the local paper caught my eye: 'Local man dies in freak accident.'
With a sinking heart I bought a copy and sat on a park bench to read it. It appeared that Karol Krovic had been found dead in his van down a quiet country lane, apparently from a heart attack. His van had swerved off the road and ended up in a ditch. Weirdly, on the seat next to him, was a life-sized plastic skeleton with a pink feather boa around its neck. The police were at a loss to understand the significance of this. But I could. He must have been on his way to another seance, of course.

So that was the end of my career as an Assistant Grief Counsellor but, in a way I wasn't too upset. It had pricked my conscience too much. Unemployed again, I felt as if bad luck seemed to follow me everywhere.

Then, out of the blue, an old school friend rang me to say he had been offered a job as a Holiday Rep. Would I like to join him?.

I asked him whereabouts and he said, 'Somewhere in Indonesia, a place called Banda Ache, a very popular resort with lots of bars and lots of girls.'

I'd never heard of it but it sounded too good to be true so I said I would love to join him, it would be fun: After all, what could possible go wrong?

Gloria Hobson

Once Bitten

Sonya followed the crowd as she exited the cinema. It was the first time she had been to see a film since her divorce and she felt very awkward. Plenty of other people went on their own but she had relied on Peter so much that she was still very self-concious, she felt as though all her confidence had evaporated.

She would have loved to call for a drink on her way home as they used to do but it was out of the question now. It wasn't as if she had enjoyed the film – some sort of French arty thing – but she could not stay at home alone any longer.

She hailed a cab as she thought it wasn't safe to walk home alone this late at night, and as her small house appeared through the gloom, she breathed a sigh of relief and scuttled inside like a frightened mouse. She must get a grip of herself or she would end up like one of those middle-aged divorcees that she had always despised.

It would take a long time for her to recover from the way things had ended, she'd had no idea anything was wrong. She came home from work one evening to find a note on the kitchen table and all his clothes and toiletries missing. Apparently he had fallen for a girl in the office, that was all the explanation he gave, he didn't even say sorry, it was as if the last few years had meant nothing to him.

Sonya was a shy girl who kept herself to herself, she had no real close friends, just some girls from work who only ever talked about fashion, make-up and men. She hadn't really needed them as Peter was her whole world, but that was gone now and for the first time in her life she felt truly alone.

Then it all changed, as is often the case. A new guy came into the Office to replace the retiring chairman. Of course, she was just a lowly receptionist, so apart from the usual 'good morning' when he came in, their paths seldom crossed. Until the annual Christmas dinner that was.

As usual that took place at a local hotel, quite a swish place, just out of town. After the meal most of the staff stayed on to enjoy a bit of dancing. The meal, as usual, was excellent and then most of the party moved to the bar area, near the small dance floor where a local DJ was setting up his equipment.

Sonya didn't usually stay and was just about to get up and head towards the cloakroom when a voice behind her said, 'Not leaving already, are you?' She turned and much to her surprise saw it was Jim Mercer, the new Chairman. Blushing slightly she said, 'yes, it's been a nice meal but I have to get off home, I'm not much of a party person.'

'Would you just have one dance with me, please, I like to meet all the staff if possible. We never get much chance at the office, everyone is so busy. Your name is Sonya, am I right?'

She couldn't get out of it without being rude so she reluctantly got up and moved towards the dance floor. Thank goodness they were only playing some nice easy listening music, she thought, as she wasn't very good at anything too vigorous.

She sensed all eyes on her, which she hated, she really didn't like too much attention. After the dance they sat at a nearby table and he brought 2 glasses of wine from the bar.

Sonya watched him, he wasn't classically handsome, his face was too craggy, but he did have an easy charm and his slight Scottish accent helped tremendously. They talked and she tried to keep it light, but then came the bombshell. 'Is your husband baby sitting tonight?' he smiled.

Now, she thought, do I lie outright or bite the bullet and tell him the truth? She had no choice

'Actually I'm divorced Mr Mercer,' she murmured.

'I'm sorry, I didn't mean to upset you, I just noticed your wedding ring and I made the wrong assumption, I didn't mean to embarrass you.'

'That's alright,' she replied, 'But I must go now, thankyou for the drink.' She stood up and he followed her to the door.

'It's been nice talking to you, Sonya, do have a nice Christmas and I will see you in the New Year.' He left her and she stood on the doorstep waiting for a cab.

The first day back after the holiday was very strange. One of the Partners came to speak to her to ask if she had seen Mr Mercer yet and she said he had not checked in at the front desk but sometimes, if he used the rear car park, he would use the back door and by-pass her. But he was not in his office and was not answering his phone. It was not like him at all.

It was decided to send 2 members of staff to his house just in case he had been taken ill but there was no sign of him, his car was in the garage but the door was locked so, reluctantly, the police were called and a thorough search of the house was made, but everything seemed to be in order. It was a mystery.

It was about this time that Sonya's nightmares began. At first they were quite brief and didn't make much sense. She was a poor sleeper anyway, one more sign of her loneliness perhaps. People at work started to notice how tired she looked so she tried to hide the dark rings around her eyes with extra make up.

One particular night she woke up screaming and had to go downstairs for a cup of camomile tea, hoping it would settle her. She tried to remember her dream, something about a dark, creepy forest, a man who looked very familiar but couldn't quite place and someone really scary wearing a strange dark mask. An owl hooted nearby and there was a strange smell of decay, like rotting leaves. It was very unsettling.

The next day as she walked into the office, she was alarmed to see two policemen talking to one of the Partners. A sudden fear gripped her and she felt quite faint.

'Ah, Sonya, I mean Mrs Parker,' said Tony, one of the juniors. 'These policemen would like a word with you. Will you come up to my office? It will be more private, I'll get someone else to man the front desk for a while.'

They trooped upstairs and entered a small office with a window overlooking the car park where she could see a police van and three uniformed officers hanging about. 'Right, Mrs Parker, I'm Detective Sergeant Welsh, I'll get straight to the point,' he said. 'We've had a report about a missing person,' he looked down at his notes. 'Mr Jim Mercer. Apparently he hasn't been seen for some days which we understand is completely out of character. We are speaking to everyone, of course. Did you know him well?'

'Not particularly,' she replied, 'just to say 'Good Morning', that's all. Where do you think he could be?'

'That's what we are trying to establish,' he replied. 'Tell me, did you ever see him away from the Office?'

'No, I never mix with anyone from work,' Sonya said, not liking the way this was going.

'How about the Christmas meal at the Albany?' he persisted.

'What about it?' she snapped, 'we just chatted for a few minutes, that's all.' This is all down to the office gossip, she thought, people read far too much into things.

'And you haven't seen him since?' he asked

'No, certainly not,' Sonya replied, 'I really don't know anthing about him, I don't even know if he is married or not.'

'Well, actually, it was his estranged wife who reported it,' the Sergeant replied.

'I wish there was something I could tell you that would help, but I'm afraid I can't.' Sonya stood up to leave.

'If you think of anything please let us know.' He gave her a card and she hurried from the room feeling quite angry - why should she know any more than the other people who work here, she thought? Just because we had one dance and one drink at the Christmas party.

About a month later came the news we had all been dreading, a body had been found in a forest about 20 miles away, not yet officially identified but it was said to be a well dressed man in his forties. The police visited us again and the news became official, he had been identified by his brother who had come down from Scotland at their request. The body was not suitable for his wife to see.

At first Sonya and the rest of the staff thought it must have been a suicide but the Post Mortem put paid to that. His hands had been tied behind his back and a bullet wound was found at the back of his head. A Rolex watch was also missing. Murder was evident.

The staff were all shocked and upset even though he hadn't been with us for very long, so it was decided to close for a few days, partly as a mark of respect and partly because it would be impossible to concentrate on anything at the moment. Of course, the office gossip went into over drive with all sorts of outrageous theories, but one thing that did emerge was that his marriage had been on the rocks, his wife had recently left him for a guy who worked in the same office as herself.

Sonya took all of this in of course, and thought how strange that his own marriage had crumpled in a similar way to her own. How strange was that?

A few days later – on a Sunday - she had a surprise phone call from her ex. He wanted to collect some books and CD's he had left behind. Although she would have preferred not to see him again, it would be churlish to say no, so she asked him to call about 6.00 o'clock. She collected all the items and put them in a cardboard box so she could hand them over with as little conversation as possible.

He pulled up promptly in a rather battered old Lada. There was a girl in the front passenger seat. He seemed strangely subdued and a little nervous as he came in.

'How are you?' he asked politely.

'I'm coping, just about,' she said, on the brink of tears.

'OK, thanks for these,' and he picked the box up, looking at his watch. ' I must go, we're running late,' and he almost ran down the garden path to his girlfriend who was glaring at me out of the car window.

How strange, she thought, he didn't look at all well, he'd lost weight and he seemed a bit down-at-heel. The Lada wasn't his style at all, he usually preferred something more up-market. Perhaps they had fallen on hard times, she thought rather childishly, serves them right.

The police investigation picked up speed now that murder was confirmed, who could hate him so much? He seemed very personable to

Sonya but, of course, you never knew what went on in people's private lives. Why was his body found in a forest far away? We might never know.

There were no signs of a struggle in the house or any blood stains any where so the assumption was that he was killed in situ and an attempt made to hide the body.

Meanwhile, Sonya had troubles of her own. The nightmares had returned with a vengeance so she went to see her GP who said it was probably a combination of worries about her divorce and the murder investigation, a course of tranquilisers should help. He also gave her a week off work.

They eased slightly but did not go away entirely. She wondered if the forest in her dream had anything to do with the murder but they had started long before Jim's body had been found.

Could it have been a portent? Surely not, she didn't really belive in that sort of thing. But who was the person in the mask? She would probably never know.

Later, her mind wandered back to the recent visit of her ex. She wondered why he had been in such a hurry, he kept looking at his watch, obviously his friend in the car was getting impatient. Then Sonya was struck by something she should have noticed at the time, how could she not have seen it? The watch was a Rolex, she was quite sure, they were very distinctive and she remembered that Peter had always coveted one but had never had the money.

It was silly, just a coincidence surely? He could have got it anwhere, perhaps it was a gift from his new lady friend or he'd bought a second hand one. Yes, that was it surely.

Nevertheless, it did worry her, what about his new girlfriend, who was she? Had she anything to do with it? No, of course not, it must be the new medication making her paranoid.

Then the Coroner finally released the body and a date was set for the funeral. All the staff were to attend.

The Chapel of Rest was packed, friends, family, lots of work colleagues from the many companies he had worked for over the years. He was a vary popular man, it seemed.

Sonya looked around. At the front sat the grieving widow, beautifully dressed in an expensive black, woolen suit with a matching cloche hat with very fine lace hiding her face. Very stylish. Sat next to her was the brother who had identified Jim's body.

Afterwards, the mourners gathered outside to admire the beautiful floral tributes, gradually getting in their cars either to go home or go on to the wake. Out of the corner of her eye, tucked away behind some trees, she saw a familiar looking car – a Lada. Peter was leaning out of the window. Mrs Mercer walked quickly towards him and gave him a passionate kiss on the mouth. Sonya could hardly believe her eyes, most everyone else had gone so no one else had witnessed it.

Suddenly someone tapped her on the shoulder and she jumped. It was Daisy, one of the secretaries from work. 'Do you want a lift back into town, Sonya?' she asked.

'Yes, but look what I've just seen over there,' she replied, pointing, but as she turned the Lada was just pulling away. 'Never mind,' she said, 'let's go.'

That night Sonya sat in her lounge trying to digest everything that had happened that day. What exactly had she seen? Obviously, her ex was having an affair with Jim Mercer's widow (the girl in the office he'd told her about). Had they anything to do with his death she wondered or was it just a co-incidence? She remembered the Rolex and she thought about her dreams. Who was the person in the mask? And then she thought, what if it wasn't a mask, what if it wasn't a mask but a black cloche hat with fine lace hiding the face? Yes, it was a possibility but what could the motive have been? They do say most murders are committed for greed or passion, or both.

Peter didn't have much money after his own divorce, hence the Lada, but Jim would have been a wealthy man and that could have been a good enough motive. I'll speak to the police in the morning, she thought and leave it with them.

She went to bed that night and for the first time in ages, did not have a single nightmare.

The next day Sonya sat in a draughty office in the local Police Station talking to an Inspector Smythe. Slowly and carefully she told them everything she knew, she realised a lot of it was hearsay but there were always fingerprints and DNA testing that could be carried out.

It took almost 2 hours to get everything on tape and she was completely drained when she was finished. Inspector Smythe thanked her and seemed to think there was enough there to warrant further investigation. What he didn't tell her was that they already had their suspicions and they had been running some tests of their own. It's a well known fact that most murders are commited by someone known to the victim.

Faced with all the evidence, Peter broke down and seemed quite relieved to get it all off his chest. He blamed his girlfriend, Lois, for everything, she was the instigator. She had asked her husband for a divorce and he had refused. He also refused to give her any money: 'You've made your bed, now lie in it,' was his reponse.

So, they hatched a plan. They went to his house and forced him at gunpoint into their car. They drove to the forest and marched him to a secluded spot where they shot him in the back of the head, a cold-blooded murder. They then covered his body with some leaves and just left him there to rot.

Lois then assumed that, after the required length of time, he would be declared dead and, as his widow, she would get all his money. It sounded like a simple plan and it might have worked if Sonya had not been haunted by those awful dreams. She felt sure that Jim had been trying to communicate with her.

At the trial it was confirmed that Peter's fingerprints were found in Jim's house and the gun was found in the boot of the Lada. They must have felt so confident with their plan that they didn't make much of an effort to cover their tracks.

Sonya didn't attend Court as she had no wish to see either of them. Faced with all the evidence, the pair had no choice but to plead guilty as they stood in the dock together. A life sentence for both with a recommendation they serve at least 25 years was the predicted verdict.

Gloria Hobson

Naturally, Sonya was the talk of the office, which she hated, of course. She eventually decided to move to pastures new and make a fresh start. She met a very nice man at an art class she enrolled on at the local College. He was a widower but she wanted to take things slowly.

'Once bitten, twice shy,' as they say.

The Vampyres of Montevideo and Other Strange Tales

The Doppleganger

It started as a normal day for Martin, a busy day at the Bank, a quick lunch, home for 5.00 and tea at 6.00 He lived with his mother in a modest house in a small market town in North Yorkshire. At one time he had had his own little flat in the town but when his father died suddenly five years ago, he moved back home, mostly to keep his mother company. Generally they rubbed along pretty well.

They were creatures of habit, a little set in their ways, some would say. After tea he would sit and read, maybe watch a little television or listen to music. His mother liked to knit.

At the weekend they would sometimes ride out to the coast or the countryside and maybe have lunch at a nice country pub.

It may have started as a normal day but that was soon to change. 'Were you ill today?' asked his mother over tea.

'No, why?' he replied, slightly puzzled.

'Well, Mrs. Portree said she saw you at the Doctors at about 10.00 clock.'

'It wasn't me,' Martin said, ' I never left the Bank all day.'

'She was sure it was you, she even said, *Hello Martin, don't see you here very often.* And you said you were collecting a prescription for me.'

Well, that was how it started, it was puzzling but not particularly worrying and he had almost forgotten about it until, one Monday lunch time he walked into his usual sandwich shop and asked for a ham roll.

'What, another already?' smiled Sally, the assistant.

'What do you mean?' asked Martin.

'Well, you called about 20 minutes ago for the same thing, you must be very hungry.'

Rather than stand and argue about it, Martin walked out, confused as to what it could mean. There must be someone in the town with a striking resemblance to himself which he found disconcerting rather than frightening.

The next few days passed normally and the events of the last few days gradually faded from his mind. His mother was going away for a few days to stay with Hannah, an old school friend who lived near Whitby, so he would have the house to himself, which he quite liked now and again.

On the Monday morning he arrived at the Bank at about 8.50, his usual time, to be greeted with astonished looks. 'Is there a problem?' he asked Philip, his chief clerk.

'Well, yes and no, I had a call to say you had had a bad fall and broken your leg so you would not be coming in today. It must be someone's idea of a sick joke.'

Martin was astonished and somewhat annoyed. Whoever this was, it was getting beyond a joke, but what could he do? He could hardly go to the police, they would think he was mad.

The rest of the day passed without any further incidents. He returned home to an empty house to find a pile of post behind the door, all addressed to him of course, all identical. They were demands for money, mostly overdue utility bills, completely false, of course. One thing Martin did pride himself on was never being late with any sort of payments. In a fit of rare temper, he tore them all up and threw them in the fire.

So far Martin had treated recent events with a kind of bemused patience but this latest matter was the last straw. He decided ro ring one of his old workmates, recently retired, to see if he could offer any advice. They agreed to meet at his local, so after a quick shower and a change of clothes, he left to walk the short distance to the Red Lion. His friend,

Derek, was waiting for him and had already ordered two whiskies. It was very cosy near the open fire and still fairly quiet, it would be buzzing later as it filled up with locals.

Feeling a little foolish, Martin told Derek about all the strange incidents of the past week, expecting, any minute, for his friend to break out laughing. But, to his surprise, he did no such thing.

Sipping at his drink, Derek asked him if he was familiar with the word 'doppelganger'?

Martin replied that he had once seen a film years ago but couldn't remember much about it.

'Well,' said Derek,' it is a German word, of course, it literally means a duplicate or double, like a sort of twin – an evil twin that is. They do say everyone has a double somewhere in the world.'

'Is it something I need to be worried about, I mean, can it be dangerous? asked Martin nervously.
'I'm not usually a believer in the supernatural.'

'There are various things you need to be aware of, for instance if someone else sees it, it can mean a possible serious illness for you. If you see one yourself it can be a portent of your own death. Apparently it is said that American President Abraham Lincoln saw one just before he was assassinated. Sorry, not very cheerful, I know.'

'Well, you've certainly given me plenty to think about,' Martin said, 'do you really believe all that yourself?'

'I try to keep an open mind,' said Derek enigmatically, 'but it does seem very strange, just because you have a double somewhere doesn't neccesarilly mean it is malicious, of course. Try not to worry too much. Let's order another drink and talk about the footie instead, shall we?'

Back home, Martin went over all that his friend had told him. Surely there must be a more rational explanation. But the thought that it could be malicious did nothing to calm his nerves and he went to bed that night feeling very uneasy.

Next day was a Friday and the Bank closed at noon. He needed a few provisions for the weekend so he headed for the local market where he wandered aimlessly about the colourful stalls. He bought some fruit and then his eye was caught by a stall selling antiques, bric-a-brac, that sort of thing.

In the corner, near the back, was a small statuette, it was about a foot high and made of spelter. It looked a little like a figure out of a Grimms Fairy Tales book, a sort of evil elf. The stall holder came over.

'Unusual, aint it mate?' he growled. 'New in, supposed to ward off evil spirits, so they say, if you believe that sort of thing.'

Well, normally, Martin would have walked away but he hesitated. 'Where did you get it from?' he asked.

'A job lot from the Continent, mostly Germany, I think. I can do you a good price if you are interested.' So, after a little haggling, they agreed on a price and Derek returned home with the strange looking figure wrapped up in brown paper.

After tea, he decided to give the figure a clean and soon he had it shining beautifully and he placed it on the chest of drawers in his bedroom. Feeling silly he spoke out loud. 'I don't know who you are but can you please protect me from this Doppelganger who is making my life a misery.' There was no response, of course, just a baleful stare.

That night he slept well and woke up feeling quite refreshed. With a spring in his step he decided to do a spot of gardening. The small gate at the front of the house opened on to the road that led into town. Every hour a bus passed by and the passengers would look across, as people do. He was used to it and it didn't really bother him.

As he pruned some roses he heard a bus approaching and he straightened up, his back tweaking a bit.
Suddenly, his heart missed a beat and he felt all the colour drain out of his face. Looking back at him, from a rear window, staring directly, was a face that was very familiar – his own! Grinning evilly and nodding like one of those silly little dogs that some people have in the back window of their cars.

The Doppleganger! He stared as the bus sped past towards the town.

So, he really did exist, but what did it want? He thought hard, what could he do to stop this nonsense? He went back inside to his bedroom and picked up the 'ELF' as he called him.

'Come on, you,' Martin hissed, 'earn your keep.' He carried him outside into the garden and waited for the next bus to appear. Nervously he stood by the low wall until he heard the distant rumble as the bus approached. He readied himself and held the ELF. As the bus drew level he could see the Doppelganger smirking at him. He sat the figurine on the wall and the Doppelganger saw it straight away. He tried to pull back in his seat and Martin stared as a bright light flashed suddenly. He blinked and when he looked up again the Doppelganger was nowhere to be seen.

It had worked! He ran back inside, he could hardly believe it. He poured himself a whiskey to steady his nerves, he would ring his friend Derek and tell him the good news. He picked up the ELF and took him back upstairs. The relief was overwhelming and a flood of gratitude passed through him.

The rest of the weekend passed peacefully, he felt the best he had felt for ages. His mother would be back on Sunday evening so he had better tidy up and clear away all the dirty dishes that had accumulated in her absence.

He was sitting in his chair reading a newspaper and drinking some tea when he heard the front door open. 'Hello, Martin, are you there?'

'Yes, I'm in here Mother,' he called back, as she opened the door.

He put his paper down as she came in and bent down to kiss the top of his head. As she looked in his eyes, her face paled and she pulled back in horror, a scream welling up in her throat at the travesty that was once her son. She passed out in sheer terror.

'Don't get too upset,' he said gently, 'you'll soon get used to me. I'm just the evil twin you didn't know you had. I think we'll rub along quite nicely once you get to know me.' He was pleased with his new position, it would suit him very well until he felt the need to move on, as all good doppelgangers must eventually, and he sipped contentedly at his tea.

Gloria Hobson

The Army of Lost Souls

The bombardment was unceasing, terrifying, deadly. A huge shell burst overhead, sending rocks, trees and body parts raining down into the shallow crater where young Jimmy was sheltering. He huddled as close as he could to his dead comrades, burrowing under the tangle of arms and legs, oblivious to the stench and the blood oozing over him, conscious only of the need to survive – if it was possible to survive this hell-hole.

He could feel the ground tremble under him and out of the corner of his eye he spotted a huge rat feasting on some entrails. He turned away, nauseous; the crows would be next. As soon as there was a break in the bombardment they would descend like vultures, huge black wings flapping as they squabbled over the tastiest morsels. And God knows, there were plenty.

It seemed like only yesterday when he had kissed his tearful mother goodbye and headed off with his brother to the nearby town to join the queue of other young men answering Lord Kitchener's call to arms. He was only fifteen but he was big and strong after years working on the family farm, it was easy to lie, no questions were asked. The Recruiting Sergeant was keen to get his quota and they were soon in the back of a truck with other youthful recruits heading off to a training camp on the east coast.

And now, here he was, in the nightmare that was the Western Front, desperate to stay alive. A slight breeze came across no-mans-land and with it, a faint smell of mustard.

Gas! thought Jimmy in terror.

If he made a dash for it he would surely be shot down. He tore a shirt off a nearby corpse, urinated on it and knotted it around his face like a scarf. A Corporal had given him this tip, but he didn't know if it would work; if death came he just hoped it would be quick and painless.

After a few minutes he opened his eyes. It all seemed very still and quiet. The shelling had stopped, thank God !

Jimmy moved cautiously from under the bodies and peered over the rim of the shell hole. He could neither see nor hear any movement, just the faint call of a lark high above him. He crawled out and looked around, there was a slight incline to his left with a few tree stumps jutting out and what looked like the remains of a farmhouse; only a pile of rubble but it would offer some cover and a better view of his surroundings.

Feeling very weak he pulled himself over the rocky ground, past the remains of men and equipment, expecting any minute for the bombardment to re-start, but there was nothing.

Perhaps the enemy had had enough of this ceaseless, senseless slaughter. He knew had.

Wearily, he clambered up the slope and finally slumped down with his back against a wall. Looking up he could see a deep blue sky and a brilliant sun, it was going to be a beautiful summers' day.

Suddenly he heard a rustling behnd him and he grabbed his rifle. Then he heard a familiar voice:

'Hello Jim. What's happened to you?' It was his brother.

'Sam!' exclaimed Jimmy with relief, 'what are you doing here? I thought your unit was 50 miles away.'

'We were, but we were all wiped out last night, they trapped us and a gas attack finished us off.'

'Were you the only survivor? asked Jimmy, in amazement.

'No, Jim, we all died.'

'But, I don't understand,' said Jimmy, his voice trembling slightly.

Sam took him gently by the shoulder and turned him around.

'Look down there where you were sheltering, what do you see?'

Gloria Hobson

Jimmy looked back at the shellhole. He could make out Corporal Smythe with his red hair and the Sergeants stripes were visible on what remained of his body.

Just underneath was another corpse which looked familiar; a stocky lad with rosy cheeks who almost appeared to be sleeping.

'It's you, Jimmy,' said Sam. 'But don't be afraid, we can go together, that's why I came looking for you.'

And he put his arm around him and together they walked forward, into the sunlight, towards a field of scarlet poppies……..

A Silver Lining

It started off, like most things do, as a normal day, but I would look back on this amd realise life was never going to be the same again.

To give you some background; My name is Imogen and I am 22. I was orphaned as a child when both my parents were killed in a road accident. My Aunt Caroline, my mother's sister, took me in and brought me up, for which I will be forever grateful.

She was a divorcee who had been married to a very wealthy man so I had quite a privileged upbringing, I went to a nice private school and then on to Uni, where I studied History and Art.

As well as a nice townhouse, my Aunt also owned a small cottage in North East Scotland, in a small fishing village near Aberdeen, which she sometimes rented out. We would go there ourselves two or three times a year, it was very peaceful, quite near the harbour and the people were very friendly.

I would take my sketch pad with me as I loved to go down to the harbour and sketch all the fishing boats bobbing about and all the activity that was going on especially as a catch came in.

My best friend, who I met at Uni, was a girl called Sally who would sometimes come and stay with me during the holidays. On this particular day my Aunt had gone to Scotland to give the cottage a good Spring clean in readiness for the Summer season and Sally had arrived to keep me company for a few days. We'd just had lunch and were preparing to go out and do some shoppong when the phone rang.

'That'll be my Aunt,' I said, smiling, 'checking up on me.' It wasn't, it was the sort of phone call we never want to get.

'Good day, am I speaking to Miss Imogen Jefford?' said a man with a very pronounced Scottish accent.

'Yes,' I replied, 'who is this?'

'I'm Inspector McDonald of the Grampian Constabulary, I'm afraid I have some bad news for you. Your Aunt,' and he paused as if looking at his notes, 'Mrs Caroline Beaumont, has been found dead in her cottage. I'm sorry to break this news to you, I realise it must be a shock to hear something like this,' he said.

'Was it an accident?' I asked, my voice trembling slightly

'Well, from the initial examination by the Police Doctor, it would seem she had a heart attack. She was found sitting in a chair in the lounge. She would probably have known very little about it, if that's any consolation.'

'Where is she now?' I asked

'She's been taken to the Mortuary at the local hospital, but I'm afraid I'm going to have to ask you to come and formally identify her,' he said.

'Yes, of course,' I replied, looking at my watch. 'I don't think I can make it today, will tommorow be allright, it's nearly 300 miles and I don't fancy driving in the dark?'

'That's fine, if you like I can meet you at the cottage, just give me a ring when you're 30 minutes away and I can take you to the Hospital myself. Once again, my sincere condolences.'

So that was that, just out of the blue your life can change, I felt as though I had been orphaned all over again. The rest of the day was a bit of a blur, Sally agreed to come with me so we packed a few things, I imagined we might have to stay for a few days. I rang a friend of my Aunt's from the Book Circle she had recently joined and asked her to pass on the news. I said I would be in touch as soon as I knew the funeral arrangements.

We set off next day at 8.30, had a quick lunch at a service station just outside Newcastle and arrived at the cottage at about 3.00. Inspector McDonald was waiting for us, standing next to a Police Land Rover, enjoying the view. It was a beautiful day and quite a few people were admiring the harbour down below in the Spring sunshine.

We popped into the house with our luggage and then joined him in the Land Rover for the ride to the hospital, he said he would prefer to take us and bring us back as he thought we had done enough driving for one day. The County Hospital was a good 30 minutes away and when we arrived, we were escorted directly to the mortuary. I braced myself for the task ahead. As the shroud was lifted, I gasped in shock and almost fainted, the assistant managed to catch me and I was helped in to a chair.

'Can you confirm that this is your Aunt, Caroline Beaumont?' asked the Inspector.

I paused to compose myself. 'NO! That is not my Aunt, I have no idea who that is!' There was a stunned silence. 'I've never seen that woman in my life. There must have been a dreadful mistake.' And I burst into tears.

Instead of returning to the cottage, we went straight to the Police Station. Sally tried to comfort me as best she could. We were ushered into an interview room where some tea was brought in to us by a female Officer, as we tried to get to grips with these strange events.

'So, you are telling me that the woman in the Mortuary is definitely not your Aunt?' Inspector McDonald asked.

'Definitely , my friend Sally will back me up, she spends a lot of time at my house, don't you?'

Sally nodded and squeezed my hand comfortingly.

'I just can't understand it, who is she and why is she wearing my Aunt's clothes and jewellery? What was she doing in my Aunt's house and, more importantly, where is my Aunt?'

'Could she be a friend who was visiting, or a neighbor perhaps? He queried.

'My Aunt didn't spend a lot of time up here and when she did, it was usually with me. The only reason she was here now is because the usual cleaner who looks after the cottage, has gone to New Zealand to visit relatives. Her name is Mrs Platt and she lives a few doors down. She cleans the cottagel between lets, changes the bedding and so on. She has a key so she can let guests in,' I explained.

'Well, we will speak to her family, of course, see if they have seen anything suspicious,' the Inspector said, 'there's a lot for us all to puzzle over. I must ask you now, in view of these new developments, if you would mind moving into a hotel for a few days while we carry out a full forensics investigation, fingerprints, DNA etc. I'm sorry for any inconvenience. WPC Brown here,' he nodded at the police woman, 'will run you home to collect your things, try not to touch anything please. And please give your keys to her. Thankyou for all your help, we will be in touch.'

We were ushered out, it was already dark and after we had picked up our cases, I gave the keys to WPC Brown, who smiled at us sympathetically. 'I'm sure there will be a simple explanaton for it all,' she said in parting.

So, we drove to a Holiday Inn on the outskirts of town and booked in. We had a quick drink at the bar and decided to have an early night, we had had enough for one day.

Next morning, we were still confused. I said to Sally, 'why did the dead woman have my Aunt's clothing on, do you think?'

'Do you think it could be someone she befriended or felt sorry for and took her in?'

'Yes, but it's just not like her, she always said 'Charity begins at home', she didn't mind giving donations to worthy causes but she would never invite a total stranger into her home.'

So we hit a bit of a hiatus, hanging about in the hotel then going for a walk in the local park, even going to the cinema one night, anything to pass the time. After two or three days the police rang to say we could return to the cottage, they had completed their enquiries for the time being.

WPC Brown left the keys at the front desk, we settled our bill and drove a little nervously back to the harbourside.

As we walked through the front door we got a bit of a shock, everywhere was covered in the white powder they use for fingerprinting and all the furniture had been moved around and even the bedding had been disturbed. All through the house was that sickly smell of decay, after all, a dead body had lain there for quite a while. Apparently that was what had first caught the attention of the postman who could smell something unpleasant through the letter box. He'd then peered through the window, saw the woman in the chair, and immediatelty called the police.

So we opened all the doors and windows and spent the rest of the day giving the cottage a full deep clean until finally we could relax, although we had to move the chair where the body had been and drag it into the back yard to be taken away.

A week later there was a knock at the door and there stood Inspector McDonald. 'Good Morning.' he smiled, 'I've got some news you might be interested in, we've identified the dead woman.' He sat down and Sally went into the kitchen to make some tea.
'It turns out she was what you might call the local bag lady. We put a description in the local paper and a few people came forward. We found one old man who was willing to come to the mortuary and he confirmed her name was Elsie. He didn't know her last name but she'd been around time for quite a while. She could be a bit of a nuisance at times, begging and so on.'
'Well, I'm pleased to hear that but I still cannot understand how she came to be here.' I replied. 'My Aunt wasn't the kind of woman to invite someone like that into her house.'
'No, I agree, but I do have a bit of a theory,' he said and we left it at that.

The next day Sally told me she would have to return home as her mother had to go into hospital for a routine operation and she was needed to look after her younger siblings. So, I ran her to the local station and waited till her train arrived and waved her goodbye. I wished I could go with her but I had to stay a little bit longer.

As I opened the door, I could see an envelope on the doormat, no stamp, so it must have been hand delivered. I made a coffee and sat down to read it. This is what it said:

Gloria Hobson

Dear Miss Jefford,

I have heard about your Aunt's disappearance and felt I had to let you know something. A month ago, on the 17th to be exact, my husband and I went to a hotel near Stonehaven to celebrate my sister's 50th birthday. As we sat at our table I glanced around the room and saw your Aunt, who I knew by sight, with a very smartly dressed middle aged man – a bit of a silver fox you could say. They were, for want of a better word, canoodling. Nothing wrong with that of course. Then later, as we were leaving, I stood in the lobby with my sister and watched the two of them waiting by the lift, obviously going up to their room for the night. I'm not criticising, they are both adults, but I just thought you might want to know. Maybe the police can check this out for you.

The letter wasn't signed but obviously must be from someone local so I rang the Inspector and whithin half an hour he was at my door. He sat on the settee to read it and I agreed that he should take it with him so see if the writer could be traced.

'You said the other day that you had a theory, what is it?' I asked.

'Well,' he began, 'suppose Elsie – the deceased – knocked at your door to ask for money or food, found it unlocked and let herself in. She had something to eat and the fell asleep. When she awoke it
was dark and the house was silent. So, she went upstairs to see if she could find any valuables, tried on your Aunt's clothes, went back downstairs and fell asleep again. Then, unfortunately, she had a fatal heart attack sometime during the night. What do you think?'

'Yes, it sounds very plausible but what about my Aunt?' I asked.

'Now that we have this letter, if it turns out that their stay at the hotel coincides with Elsies' death, it looks as though she never returned home. So, we need to find this man and do some checking up, I'll
 be in touch. By the way, where's your friend Sally?'

'She had to go home, her mother's ill, so I don't know if she'll be able to come back for a while,' I said.

'Will you be alright on your own, especially in this house?' he asked.

I smiled. 'I've plenty of studying to keep me occupied and I don't believe in ghosts, if that's what you're thinking.'

'Just make sure you lock all your doors and ring if anything happens to alarm you,' and with that he left and I watched the Land Rover pull away. I wonder if he's married I thought, shamelessly, he's very handsome and he's not got a ring on his finger.

The next morning, about 10.00 clock, there was a heavy knock at the door. I looked cautiously through the peephole to see a very smart, middle aged man, looks like a salesman, I thought, I'll try to get rid of him. I opened the door.

'Oh, Hello,' he seemed surprised, 'Is Caroline at home?' he enquired. I was so shocked it must have shown on my face.

'Who are you?' I managed to ask.

'I'm Gerald, oh, hang on, I bet you're Imogen aren't you? She talks about you all the time' he smiled. 'Will she be long?'

'You'd better come in,' I said and he folowed me into the lounge.

I went to make some tea while he made himself comfortable on the settee.

'This cottage is so cosy.' he commented. 'Always so very warm and friendly, have you been here long, I don't want to disturb you if you're busy.'

'I'm afraid I have some bad news,' I said and I told him everything I knew, well almost everything. I'll ring the police as soon as he's gone, I thought. But he pre-empted me.

'I'll go straight to the police and explain everything,' he said.

I told him to ask for Inspector McDonald.

'I can hardly believe it,' he said, his eyes filling with tears. 'Let me explain, my name is Gerald Rowling and I've known your Aunt for about six months. The last time I saw her was in Stonehaven, where we spent a few days together before I flew out to Singapore on business, I just got back yesterday. I can't understand it, she seemed perfectly norman and happy. I was very fond of her.' He sipped his tea. 'Do you have any idea what might have happened to her?'

'None at all,' I repied cautiously. 'It's very baffling. There was nothing here to indicate foul play and I'm sure she wasn't suicidal.'

'Oh, I agree with you, we were very happy together, in fact I was thinking of making it more permanent, but this changes everything, of course.' He stood up. 'Thank you for the tea,' he said, holding out his hand, 'I'll go straight to the police station and see your Inspector McDonald. '

He pulled out his wallet. 'Here's my card, if you need to speak to me, please give me a ring.' He drove away in a very smart Black Rover.

I sat thinking, something he said rang a bell but I couldn't quite put a finger on it so I rang Inspector McDonald and told him about my visitor and said he was on his way to see him. He said he'd watch out for him and get back to me.

I went for a walk around the harbour, sat on a wall and did a few sketches, this usually calmed me down. The sky began to darken and I felt a few spots of rain so I hurried back to the cottage. As I opened the door, the phone was ringing. It was the Inspector. 'Mr Rowling didn't arrive,' he began, 'did he come back to see you.'

'I've only just got back myself,' I explained, 'I thought he would have seen you by now, he seemed anxious to clear things up with you.'

'What did you think of him?' he asked.

'Well, he seemed very nice, very urbane, a bit of a charmer you might say. He said he was about to propose to my Aunt,' I replied. 'Why, is there a problem?'

'Right, now listen to me very carefully Imogen, I want you to lock both doors and if there's any furniture you can drag in front of them, do that now!'

'You're frightening me,' I cried. 'What is it?'

'Just do as I say, we'll be there as fast as we can.' and the line went dead.

I went to lock the doors as instructed and, as I tried to pull the settee across the room, I heard a slight noise from upstairs and my heart missed a beat, who could it be ? Then I heard the squeak of a loose floorboard coming from the top of the stairs. Someone was coming down but how had the got in? I could only think of one person – Gerald Rowling. Then I remembered what it was that had puzzled me earlier, he said he had just returned from Singapore but it had all been on the news : a serious fire in the terminal had closed it down for some weeks and the backlog was horrendous, even nearby airports were overwhelmed. So, he had lied and that was why he hadn't been to the police station.

I went into the kitchen and bent down to look under the sink where I knew I'd recently seen a hammer. As I stood up I sensed a slight movement behind me and suddenly I felt a terrible pain and everything went black.

The next thing I could remember was a familiar voice: 'Imogen, Imogen, are you alright?'

I struggled to sit up but was pushed back down gently.

'Keep still, the ambulance is on its way.' It was Inspector McDonald, he seemed very concerned as he looked down at me. I put my hand up to my head and winced, it came away covered in blood and I felt sick.

'What happened?' I mumbled, feeling very confused and I lapsed again into unconciousness.

Some very bright lights woke me up and I could see two nurses adjusting the drip-feed apparatus nearby. 'Ah, Imogen, you're back with us, are you?' one said, smiling.

'Where am I,' I asked feeling very confused.

'County Hospital.' she replied. 'You've had a nasty blow to your head but you'll be fine in a couple of days. Please try to rest now.'

The next day I awoke to see Inspector McDonald gazing down at me. 'How are you?' he asked.

'Got a bit of a headache' I said, smiling. 'I can't remember much. What really happened, was it Rowling?'

'Yes, but luckily for you, we managed to break in before he could do too much damage,' he replied.

'You do know he was lying about being in Singapore?' I said.

'Yes, we checked the flights, there are none at all at the moment, that's when the penny dropped and I realised you were in great danger. I think we broke all the speed limits to get there. I'm so glad we made it in time.'

'Did he get away' I asked worriedly.

'Only as far as the harbour, our police dog – Alfie- soon caught up with him. He's in a cell now, waiting to be charged, the man I mean, not the dog,' and he smiled thinly at his attempt at humour.

'But what about my Aunt, do you know what happened to her?'

'Yes, well partly. I'm afraid she's dead Imogen, I'm so sorry. Apparently, he had a bit of a reputation as a ladies man, he's fleeced quite a few divorcees and widows outof there savings. I think your Aunt must have been suspicious and threatened to tell the police. They went to the south coast for a few days, near Eastbourne, to try to make things up. They were last seen heading to the cliffs at Beachy Head to take some photographs. He said she went too near the edge and tripped but I think it's safe to say she was pushed, but of course we can't prove it and her body will probably never be found. It's hard to prove murder without a body, unless there are witnesses, of course.'

So there it was, Rowling was charged with attempted murder and given a lengthy sentence.

As for me, after the statutary length of time my Aunts' death was officially recognised and I inherited both houses and a substantial amount of money. I completely renovated the cottage because I still wanted to keep it as a base for myself after I'd finished my degree course.

My dear friend Sally, got married and I was chief bridesmaid and I myself got engaged to a very handsome Police Inspector from the Grampian Constabulary and we hope to marry next year

Although this story had a tragic beginning, out of it all came a happy ending for me. I still miss my Aunt Caroline and I keep a beautiful photo of her at my bedside and I murmur a little prayer to her every night.

I remember something she always said to me when I was feeling low: 'Every cloud has a silver lining.'

How true that turned out to be.

The Vampyres of Montevideo and Other Strange Tales

ABOUT THE AUTHOR

Gloria Hobson is a retired secretary who lives in West Yorkshire with her husband Barry. She has travelled extensively throughout America, Canada, Russia and Western Europe, where she seeks inspiration for her diverse narratives. She caught the writing bug at school and has always been a lover of books. Although she has been writing short stories for a long time, this is the first occasion that she has had her work published. She would like to thank her son Mark, who is also a writer, for his encouragement and for helping her with the technical side of things, and for getting her to grips with computers and the internet.

The Vampyres of Montevideo and Other Strange Tales

Gloria Hobson

Printed in Great Britain
by Amazon